THE
CHOSEN ONE

THE
CHOSEN ONE

Carol Lynch Williams

ST. MARTIN'S GRIFFIN

NEW YORK

THE CHOSEN ONE. Copyright © 2009 by Carol Lynch Williams. All rights reserved.
Printed in the United States of America. For information, address St. Martin's Press,
175 Fifth Avenue, New York, N.Y. 10010.

www.stmartins.com

The Library of Congress has cataloged the hardcover edition as follows:

Williams, Carol Lynch.
    The chosen one / Carol Lynch Williams.—1st ed.
        p. cm.
    Summary: In a polygamous cult in the desert, Kyra, not yet fourteen, sees being
chosen to be the seventh wife of her uncle as just punishment for having read books
and kissed a boy, in violation of Prophet Childs' teachings, and is torn between facing her fate and running away from all that she knows and loves.
    ISBN 978-0-312-55511-5
    [1. Cults—Fiction.   2. Polygamy—Fiction.   3. Family life—Fiction.
4. Coming of age—Fiction.]   I. Title.
    PZ7.W65588Cgr 2009
    [Fic]—dc22

                                                          2009004800

    ISBN 978-0-312-62775-1 (trade paperback)

        First St. Martin's Griffin Paperback Edition: September 2010

            10 9 8 7 6 5 4 3 2 1

For the Cliff-hangers and

for Julie, Margaret, Rita, and Uma

But most especially

for

Christian Green

I

"*If I was going to kill the Prophet,*" I say, not even keeping my voice low, "I'd do it in Africa."

I look into Mariah's light green eyes.

She stares back at me and smiles, like she knows what I mean and agrees. Like she's saying, "Go on, Kyra. Tell me more."

I kick the toe of my sneaker into the desert sand. Even this late in the evening, with the sun sinking over my shoulder, the ground is leftover hot from the day. I can feel the heat through the soles of my shoes. Feel the heat coming up from the ground, through my tights, right under the skirt of my past-the-knees dress. There isn't even a bit of a breeze.

"I'm not sure how I'd kill him. Yet." I pause so Mariah can see I am dead serious. Then I take in a big breath of air and plow ahead. "But once he's gone, I'd drag his body right next to a termite nest. Not a thing would be left of him in three hours. There're termites in Africa that can do that. No one would ever know what happened."

Again I pause. I look off toward the setting sun that has changed the desert from orange to deep red. Not quite the color of blood, but close enough. Overhead, stars start to fill the eastern sky. Just bits of light. I shrug.

"*All* of him would be gone. *Every* speck. No evidence left."

Mariah smiles at me again and lets out a bit of baby laughter. I shift her from one hip to the other, then lean close, smelling powder and, from the desert around me, sage. I touch my lips to her face so soft and smooth. Eight months old, this baby, my youngest sister, is as sweet as new butter. And just as fat. I love her.

Oh. I love her.

"I'd kill him first for me," I say into her cheek, my lips still resting there, my eyes closed. "And then I'd kill him for you. Then I'd kill him for the rest of our sisters. And our mothers. And the other women here . . ."

"Kyra."

I jump.

2

Mother Claire's voice carries out over the sand and rock and brush that make up this part of our land surrounding the Compound. The sound is so clear and sharp and near, I worry maybe she's heard me.

"Kyra," Mother Claire calls again. She stands on the porch to her trailer, the light of her place spilling out around her. Her hands are on her hips. "I see you out there. Come inside. You know we have company coming in a few minutes. Get in here now."

"Coming," I say, but not loud at all.

Mother Claire is the mean one. She's Mariah's mother, my father's first wife. My true mother, Mother Sarah, is sick in bed with pregnancy. She would stand up to this wife, at least for me. She has before. But she can't right now because she's not well.

Mariah lets out a gurgle. In the lingering light I can see that she's sleepy. Sleepy from my swaying and the heat and my voice, maybe. She puts her head on my shoulder and lets out a big yawn.

"Lucky girl," I say. "You might sleep through this tonight."

AFTER I HELP Mother Sarah get the younger girls ready for our visitors, I check on her. She's stretched out on the sofa, her face white, her belly six-months big.

"Mother," I say. I pet her long blond hair. "Can I go out-side? Just a few minutes? Everything's done."

What I'd like to do is play the piano, bring Mozart to life for the time we have until Prophet Childs shows. But the Fellowship Hall is closed now.

Mother looks at me with eyes blue as the evening sky. "What are you going to do, Kyra?" she says.

I shrug. "Just spend a minute alone."

Mother Sarah moves up on her elbow, cocks her head like she's listening. In their room I can hear my youngest two sisters playing with their baby dolls. Laura, who is just a year younger than me, writes at the dining-room table. She's filling her journal.

"We have nearly an hour before the Prophet comes by," Laura says. "Not that I was listening to your private conver-sation." Laura grins at me. Our trailer is so small we can hear one another's thoughts.

"I'll be back when you call," I say, and my mother nods, then sinks onto the sofa and closes her eyes.

I MAKE MY WAY out to the Russian Olive trees that line the back of the Compound.

We're lucky. Our trailer is closest to these trees and I love them. I love the way they smell sweet in the spring, and I

4

love the silverish-green color of their leaves. I love that, in summer, the leaves are thick and can hide me. I love that I can be alone here. I've cut off the pokey thorns from all the lower branches on one tree.

When I did that, Mother said, "Kyra Leigh Carlson! Why in the world did you use my best Cutco knives to trim a tree? You're old enough to know better than that."

"Healthier than getting stabbed," I had said. And she clucked her tongue like a hen in the chicken coop.

What I couldn't say was, "I needed a place to breathe by myself, that's why I did it." I couldn't say, "Mother, I am almost fourteen and I haven't had one minute alone except when I'm sitting on the toilet and even then Carolina tries to get in with me and I have to hold the door shut with my foot 'cause the lock's been broken I don't know how long." I couldn't say, "Some days I need to be alone." Instead, I just shrugged.

I climb up into the leaves now and settle onto my highest branch. My dress tugs at my knees till I loosen it some.

"Thank you, Jesus," I say. And I mean those words, I do.

This visit from the Prophet has excited the family. Everyone is thrilled he's coming.

"No one's mixed up," I say. "No one but me."

There's not a mother or child in my family that doesn't honor the Prophet.

"I do, too," I say. "Sometimes."

5

But life is changing for me. I'm learning new things. I'm "getting out," I say into the evening air. I'm sure I'm the only Chosen One who has wished the Prophet dead and his body picked away by termites.

I look past the crisscrossy branches of the Russian Olive toward our settlement. I can see most everything here, if I part the leaves. The lawns of the Prophet and Apostles, the store, the Temple and the Fellowship Hall where we meet for school and Wednesday evening activities. I see it all. And nobody can see me.

"Mmm," I say, breathing deep and closing my eyes. It smells so good to be by myself here.

After a moment of resting, I open my eyes and look toward my own home, seeing some of it in my head 'cause it's too dark to make out all the details: the sparse grass and red desert dirt; the shadows of my two youngest sisters in their bedroom window. From where I sit I can see the three of Father's trailers where all my mothers live. Some nights when I sit here I can pick Father out just from his shape in front of a curtain and I know who he's staying with for that week.

This spot in this tree is mine alone. I've very nearly rubbed a bottom-shaped mark on this limb I've been up here so many times. And I've not shared my hiding place with anyone. Not even with Laura, my closest sister. This is where I can think without a baby to pat or a sick person to tend or a worry to bother. It's where I can plan and dream and hope.

6

"I love being here," I say. "I love being able to see it all and having no one see me."

A breeze rushes over the desert, rustling the leaves. It's like the tree wants me here, even though I did attack it with the Cutco.

The Temple shines like a beacon. At the Prophet's house (that place takes up more space than a whole line of trailers), lights glow at the windows. I can see some people moving there. The moon slips from behind the mountains, drowning out some of the stars.

I sit for a while, doing nothing but wondering at being alone like this, wondering at the Prophet's visit, until Mother Sarah calls my name out in a weary cry, "Kyra Leigh, come on in. We're going over to Mother Claire's place now."

"I'll be back," I tell the tree, and the leaves rustle again with the wind.

I HEAR THEIR VOICES as I get closer. I can hear the kids as they hurry to meet at Mother Claire's trailer. They laugh, someone whines, a young child cries out. Maybe one of the twins? I hurry to meet them.

Here are my brothers and sisters.

Here are my father's children.

Adam, 17.

Finn, 16.

Emily, 15.

Nathaniel, 15.

Me, almost 14.

Jackson, 13.

Robert, 13.

Laura, 12.

Thomas, 11.

Margaret, 10.

Candice, 10.

Abe, 9.

April, 8.

Christian, 6.

Meadow, 5.

Marie and Ruth, 4.

Carolina, 3.

Trevor, 2.

Foster, 1.

Mariah, 8 months.

And two more babies on the way.

WE WAIT.

All of us together. Father, all the Mothers, all of the chil-dren. We girls are dressed in our Sunday best. My brothers are dressed in church clothes, too. Their ties on, some of them crooked. My hair's braided so tight I feel a headache coming on.

"Isn't this exciting?" Mother Victoria says. "The Prophet and his Apostles coming here."

Father smiles. He pulls Trevor and Foster onto his lap and smiles.

"Maybe," Mother says, her words spilling out with hope, "maybe you have been Chosen."

Her voice is low, but it's like all twenty-four of us have heard her. Even Mariah grows quiet. We look at Mother Sarah and then at Father. Now he smiles so big it looks like his face might crack wide-open.

"Hyrum says my name's been mentioned," Father says. His cheeks have turned pink. We stare at him. "They've talked of us all in meetings."

The timer on the stove goes off and Mother Claire hurries to the oven, the heels of her shoes tapping on the linoleum. From where I sit, I can see her; the kitchen, dining room, and living room are all one place in this trailer. She pulls cookies from the oven.

Mother Victoria clasps her hands under her chin. "They've been talking of us? Are you serious, Richard?"

"That's what Hyrum says." Father squeezes a hug around the boys in his lap and one laughs. "He talked to me yesterday. Told me we'd get the visit."

9

"And he was right," Mother Claire says from the kitchen. She almost smiles.

All the sudden, I'm excited, too. Anyone can see that the Prophet and Apostles are blessed. They have real homes. They have nice cars. Maybe . . . my heart thuds with the thought . . . maybe things are changing for us. Maybe I was harsh to wish the Prophet dead.

"I've been faithful," Father says. He looks around the room at his family. He smiles still. "I've been a faithful disciple."

I am warmed to the teeth at my father's smile.

My good father.

I REMEMBER sitting on my father's lap. So small, so cute (I've seen the pictures that prove it). My hair was that whitish blondish color. The color that Carolina's is now.

I wore a dress of pale blue with pink trim. And fed Father strawberries one at a time. I snuggled my head into his neck. And he laughed and kissed my face and told me how much he loved me, his Kyra.

"*Kyra, Kyra Leigh, Leigh, Leigh,*" he sang.

"*Kyra, Kyra Leigh, Leigh, Leigh,*" I sang back. "*Kyra Kyra me, me, me.*"

And Father sang, "*Kyra Kyra you, you, you.*"

I LOOK OUT the window that faces east, out over the desert. The sky's almost black now.

Mother Sarah sits near Father, leaning against him. He pats her hand, pats my brothers in his lap. Mother Victoria keeps all the smallest children quiet by telling a story of Jesus. Mother Claire wipes down an already-clean kitchen.

Adam, my oldest brother, looks over at me like he wants to say something. Emily, who is not right in her mind and who would be the oldest sister if she were sound, wanders around the room. She touches each of us, squished in tight together, on the head. "Duck, duck, duck," but no "goose" because there is no running or playing. We're waiting for the Prophet.

We are waiting for God's Anointed.

While I watch my mothers, while I gaze at my father pink-cheeked with hope, while I listen to my siblings all around me, I am struck to the center with worry. I squeeze my eyes shut. Can Adam read my mind? Is that why he looked at me that way?

I've doomed the family. I know it right that second. It feels like someone has dumped ice all over me. It feels I am right-at-that-moment covered with snow.

My father is pure. My mothers. My brothers and sisters. Emily for sure.

11

But me.

Me!

I've planned to kill someone. No! not someone! I've planned the death of the Prophet. God's Anointed. God's Chosen.

And there's more. So much more.

Without thinking, I stand. I've got to get out of here. I've got to run. Get to my secret place so I can be alone. Get away. Maybe make them safe from my unclean thoughts. From the things I've done.

"Duck, duck, duck," Emily says. She reaches for my head.

"Sit, Kyra," Mother Claire says. She's by the sink, ringing out the washcloth. "We're waiting for God's Chosen."

"I have to go," I say. Now Nathaniel and Laura stare at me. "I forgot something."

"Kyra," Father says, "whatever it is can wait."

"No, Father," I say. I can feel my face turning red. My sins on my cheeks. There for everyone to see. "I need to leave for now. You can tell me what happens. Prophet Childs won't notice I'm not here."

"Kyra," Mother says. "Sit. Please."

And Mother Victoria, all full of gasps, says, "He notices everything. He sees everything. He'd know if you weren't with us."

"Kyra Leigh," Mother says again and her voice is soft in this room full of my family. "Be obedient to your father."

"Yes, ma'am," I say, and flop back onto the sofa. Then, under my breath, where not even the closest sibling can hear me, I whisper, "God in Heaven, forgive me. Forgive me. Forgive me." It becomes my chant.

I cannot curse this family

OKAY. It's not just the planning to kill Prophet Childs. There's more. There's lots more.

Squished between my sisters I try not to think of my sins but they are all in me. I know they are there.

First, there are the books.

FINDING THE LIBRARY was an accident.

Prophet Childs would never let one of us check out books from a public library.

"We have our beliefs," he's said. "We have our God-given freedoms. And no one is going to take that away by brainwashing *us* with Satan's teachings."

Past the edge of the Compound. Past the fences. Past the river. Off our land, headed away. That's where I was, looking off to the north and Florentin. I remember the day clear.

August 13. A late Wednesday afternoon. Hotter than fire.

So hot the spit dried up in my mouth. So hot that when I stared at the empty road my eyes felt like *they* dried up, too. My work at home with my mother and with the other mothers was done—at least for a while—the quilting and helping with the laundry and working on dinner and even piano time.

So I stood there, just *stood* there, and then I heard something coming down the road behind me, the road that eventually runs in front of our Compound.

And here comes the Ironton County Mobile Library on Wheels, rolling along, headed toward Florentin. Kicking up red dust behind it.

Why, as it got closer, a shiver went right down my arms even though it had to be a million degrees standing out there in the desert sun. The library on wheels went clunking past, coming from the south, and the man driving, clean-shaven face, ball cap pulled down low on his forehead, he nodded at me.

My heart just about leapt through the bones of my chest.

I gave the driver a look, squint-eyed because of the sun *and* his nod. Who did he think he was, nodding at me like that? I stared him right in the eye, even though the Prophet would have said it was a sin to look a Gentile in the face.

But seeing that van—that nodding driver—did something to me. I don't know what. Or why.

The next day, same time, I went there again. Rushing

14

through chores and piano practice and helping the mothers. Past the Compound. Past the fences. Past the river. Off our land. A good long ways away. I waited and waited. No truck.

So the next day and the next and the next, until a week had passed, and here comes the truck, rolling along *again*. Wednesday afternoon. Same man driving. He nodded. *Again*.

My heart thumped. I squinted. Looked him dead in the eye.

Third week he stopped.

Dust billowed up around us. I could taste the dirt. Crunched sand.

He rolled down the window. "You want a library card," he said, adjusting the ball cap he wore. It wasn't even a question.

And I nodded, like he'd done to me these past weeks.

"You can take four books out at a time," he said when I inched my way into the truck, cooled by fans and air-conditioning.

I'd never seen so many books. Never. The sight made my eyes water. I mean, tear right up.

"Four?" I said. There was that sand on my tongue, gritting between my back teeth.

"Four."

I eyed the man. Eyed the books. Stood still, my heart thumping.

15

"Maybe just one," I said.

"You could start with this," he said and handed me something from a basket near his feet. "A girl just your age turned it in on my last stop. She said she loved it. *I* loved it myself."

His last stop? Another girl? *He'd* read this book?

I took the novel from him and glanced at the cover. *Bridge to Terabithia.*

I was there just a minute and I only took the one. One, I knew, would be easier to hide.

But oh, how my life changed with his stopping. My life changed when I started reading. I was different with these sinful words.

Who was this Katherine Paterson? Who was this Jesse and Leslie? People the writer knew? I could hardly read this book fast enough.

And when I did

when I got to the end

when I got to the end and

Leslie died

and Jesse was left alone without his best friend

I cried so hard that coming in from my hiding place, my tree, the book stashed in the branches, high in the prickles, Mother Victoria said, "Where have you been, Kyra? I needed help making bread." Then she looked at my face and said, her voice all worried, "Honey, what happened?"

16

I couldn't tell her a thing. Not about Leslie or May Belle or Jesse all alone. I couldn't tell Mother Victoria a thing about drowning or running or painting.

Instead, I threw my arms around her waist and said, my head on her shoulder, crying my eyeballs out, "I love you so much, Mother Victoria."

Then I set out delivering bread to my other mothers and to Sister Allred, who just had a baby, half-crying the whole way.

MY SINS.

A plan. Books. And a boy.

There's a boy.

Oh, I am carrying the weight of what I have done. But no one seems to notice.

Mariah reaches for me. I look the other way. I'm too nervous to hold Mariah, baby Mariah.

I grip Laura's hand and try not to think of what I've done. Keep my prayer chant going.

Everyone whispers together, all dressed up on a Tuesday evening, hair smoothed with water or in braids.

Mariah, quiet, holds her hands to me still.

I get to my feet again.

"Kyra?" Father says.

Mother Sarah looks at me. "Are you feeling okay, honey?"

"I want to . . ." I stop mid-sentence. I want to what? Leave? Stay? Run? Hide? "I was thinking about playing the piano," I say. A big, fat lie. One more sin added to all that I carry.

Laura tugs on my hand and I sit down beside her again.

THERE ARE JUST a few places in the whole Compound with pianos.

Prophet Childs has a concert grand in his front room. I've seen it myself. Right through the plate-glass window. Pure white and shiny, that piano is. It *has* to be a concert grand. I bet a body could see her face in the shine of that thing. He lives in a brick house, so big it casts a long shadow on the lawn when the sun starts to set. The Apostles have houses and pianos, too. Not only does being an Apostle mean blessings from God, but blessings from the land, too. That's what they've told us, and it seems that's true.

There're three pianos in the Temple, though I've only played the one in congregation room when Sister Georgia is ill. The final two pianos sit in the Fellowship Hall. One is an old Kawai. It's my favorite.

It was there, on a Sunday morning after meetings that I

wandered up to that piano and started playing *Twinkle, Twinkle, Little Star*. Just like that. Like I was born with the song stuck in my head. I was almost four.

"Listen to her," Mother Sarah said. She ran right up to me, swooped me close, and said, "Did you hear her playing that song?"

Sister Georgia, who taught music lessons outside the Compound a long time ago, before she felt she was called to be a part of The Chosen, teaches anyone who wants to learn. My mother didn't even hesitate when I plunked out that first song ten years ago. She marched me right up to Sister Georgia and said, "My Kyra is musical. She needs teaching."

And I said, "I do."

Music carries me away. Has since I was little. I can feel notes under my skin. Feel music in my muscles. Sometimes I even dream in Mozart or Beethoven scores. In the dreams, people speak out black musical notes, not words. And I understand every bit of it, exactly what they're saying, when I dream.

"NO PIANO NOW, Kyra," Father says. And right when he says that there's a tap at the door.

"They're here," Margaret says and Mother Sarah says, "Coming to see us," and sits up straighter. She is pale and in the light of the bare bulb hanging from the ceiling I can see her face is damp with sweat. She must feel awful.

Father sets Trevor and Foster on the floor and goes to the door. Quick, I pray one more time. "Please, dear Jesus. Please."

Everyone is silent.

The only sound is Father's church shoes on the floor as he walks over to open the front door. The room has grown hot with our being together.

"Ow," Laura says.

"Sorry," I say, realizing that I'm squeezing her hand too hard. I let go.

Please, please, Jesus. I'll believe. I'll be good if you choose my father. I'll never think of killing anyone again. I swear it. I can't quite say anything about the reading and there's no time to think anything more than Joshua's name.

Father opens the door.

"Prophet Childs," he says. "Brother Fields. Brother Stephens. Welcome. Oh!" Father's voice sounds full of smiles. "Hyrum, I didn't see you back there. Come on in."

The four men move into the room. We offer our Prophet the comfortable chair and he takes it. Mother Victoria moves to the floor and sits near his feet. The other brethren, including my uncle, settle into the kitchen chairs.

"Brother Carlson," Prophet Childs says. He is thin as a tree, tall with eyes so dark they look black. His brown hair

20

is slicked back from his forehead, the comb lines visible. He smiles at us all. Lifts his hands to us. "Look at this family. Look at your heritage to the Lord, Brother Carlson."

My father nods, beaming.

"Beautiful family," the Prophet says. "Your older boys are honorable young men." He nods. "The older girls are . . ." He stops. He's looking at Emily. Our wonderful Emily. Right then I see her the way our Prophet must. I see her wide face, her slanted eyes, her smile that's almost glowing. She looks at him with so much love I cannot understand how he cannot love her back. But I know he doesn't. I've heard him say he doesn't. I've heard him condemn her.

And I know what they do to those who are not whole.

"SINNERS ARE SICK. Sinners are not complete. Sinners do not please God and are cursed," he has said in meetings.

Some of the congregation cheers. Some sing, *"Amen."* Some are quiet. *Our* family is quiet.

"The unwhole won't meet God," he says. "Those who are lacking here," tapping his head, "or here," tapping his eyes, "or here," tapping his heart, "do not qualify for the kingdom."

I know it happens. It's all part of the New Cleansing and mothers don't talk of it much. The New Cleansing is part of what's quiet around here.

Sister Janie Abbott had two baby boys. Tiny things. Not more than a pound or two. One died after an hour. But the one like Emily, he lived awhile.

Prophet Childs went to their trailer. Sister Janie wasn't but thirteen. A first wife to her husband just six years older. She cried for a long time when they said the unwhole shouldn't live. She cried, hanging on to that baby as long as she could. But at last Prophet Childs had her talked out of that tiny thing.

They did away with him.

Not sure how, but I know they did. I listened in on Mother Victoria telling Mother Sarah and Mother Claire. She whispered the whole story to my mothers while I stood in the dark of the living room, quiet in the night so they might not notice me.

"They killed that unfit baby," Mother Victoria said. Her voice was full of something. Sorrow? I waited in the dark, not moving, my skin cold prickles from her words. "Thank God, thank God, the revelation came *after* Emily was born. *This* prophet's father was nothing like *he* is."

"That's right," Mother Sarah said.

And Mother Claire said, her voice low, too, "This is a new Prophet. A new leader. A new time. He's not a thing like his father. Things were hard before. They're harder now." There was silence and then, "God is mysterious."

Prophet Childs became prophet when his father died

seven years back. The mantle was handed down to him. The line of authority going through the blood. That's what Father says. There was a big funeral when Prophet Childs's father passed.

But not even a tiny burial gathering for those two babies of Sister Janie's.

I've seen her since, great big with child again, out in the cemetery, kneeling over those two small graves that Brother Abbott dug while she stood by, alone, and watched.

NOW PROPHET CHILDS looks around the room at us. Mother Victoria wraps her arms about Emily, who says, "The Prophet. The Prophet. See him?" and lets out a laugh full of joy.

"Quiet the girl, Sister Victoria," Uncle Hyrum says. His eyebrows meet right over his nose with his unhappiness.

"Hush now, Emily," Mother Victoria says. She looks nervous, the way she glances at Uncle Hyrum and then at Brother Fields and Brother Stephens and last of all at the Prophet.

"Duck, duck, duck," Emily says.

"Shhh, shhh," Mother Victoria whispers. "Shhh for now, my sweet girl."

Emily goes quiet. But she looks me right in the eyes and

grins full on. She gives me a thumbs-up sign, and if I weren't so worried about everything, I would laugh.

"Brother Carlson," Prophet Childs says to Father, at last.

Father nods, hands clasped. His face is still pink, but there's worry near his mouth.

"I have joyous news."

Laura, sitting so still beside me, takes in a breath of air. Now she grabs my hand and squeezes.

"I've been in the belly of the Temple for some time. Thinking, praying"—he points his finger toward the lightbulb—"and talking with God. It has been revealed to me that your oldest daughter, Sister Kyra, is to wed Apostle Hyrum Carlson. She will be his seventh wife in the Lord."

The room goes dead quiet. Not one sound. I think, *Father hasn't been called after all.* And then Prophet Childs's words sink in, sink in, sink in.

Me? What? *Me* to be married? I think I have no blood. I think I have lost the ability to breathe.

"Is this not a joyous occasion?" Prophet Childs says, and Brother Stephen lets out a "Praise God from whom all blessings flow."

Uncle Hyrum looks right at me.

I feel my face burn.

"The ceremony is in four Sundays, after services," the Prophet says.

It's at that moment I find my tongue. Before my mothers,

before my father. Laura's hand is squeezing me tight and I smell body odor. I think it's me.

"What?" I say.

"In a light bright as the sun the revelation came," Prophet Childs says. He stares over our heads like he's seeing things all over again. "The two of you at the stone altar, wearing the ceremonial dress, Brother Hyrum standing, you kneeling at his feet. I saw it all. I saw it all. You have been saved for him."

Uncle Hyrum nods. "I will treat you well, Sister Kyra," he says. "We will raise children unto the Lord."

"I can't do that," I say, sick just-like-that to my stomach. I stand, Laura holding my hand so tight my fingers have gone purple. When I look into her face, I see her eyes have filled with tears. I glance at Mother Sarah. She sits up straight in her chair.

Father says, "Prophet Childs, I think there must be a misunderstanding. This man is my brother."

I shake free of Laura. Step over my brothers and sisters whose faces are pale and seem like floating balloons.

"Duck, duck, duck," Emily says.

Mariah lets out a bit of a cry. Does she feel what I feel? I turn and she reaches for me. But it's like I look at a photograph, one that changes. I see her face collapse when I back away. See her little mouth open wide. Hear her start to cry.

Brother Fields reaches for me as I try to run, grabs the

sleeve of my dress, but I slap his hand away and run out into the darkness. Mariah's voice follows me.

"Wait," someone calls. Mother Claire? Then, "Hush, baby. You hush now."

How can this be? Is it for my sins? I have punished us all for my thoughts? For the books? And Joshua?

Just like that I'll be marrying my father's brother.

Just like that I'll be marrying my own uncle.

MOTHER CLAIRE MARRIED FATHER when she was fourteen and he was seventeen.

Mother Victoria married Father when she was thirteen and he was nineteen.

Mother Sarah married Father when she was thirteen and he was twenty-one.

And now me. Me. Marrying my uncle who must be sixty, at least.

Saved for him?

OUTSIDE THE SKY has gone all dark except for the half-moon. All is quiet except Mariah's wailing—a piercing cry that causes my heart to skip a beat. I almost turn back. The air is crisp, cool, though heat still rises from the desert. My uncle! I run from my family. At first, I start toward my tree. Then I think better of it.

"I don't need a tree," I say into the dark. "I don't."

So I turn around. I head back, past my trailer, past where my family meets with the Prophet and his Apostles and the old man I'm supposed to marry. My own *uncle*.

I trip on a line of bricks that Mother Victoria set up to surround a small flower garden and fall right into her petunias with an "Oof." The sweet smell makes me sick and I think I might puke. My hands and knees hurt from the fall, and my shinbone feels like a gouge of meat has been scooped out against a brick. For a moment I hesitate. I want to cry. To howl like Mariah, who is really worked up now. But I can hear the rumble of voices from the trailer one over. Can hear one of the men say, "She'll learn her place," and another say, "God's will."

I push to my feet, and hurry away, right to the biggest sin of my life. I go to Joshua's place.

THE FIRST TIME I really noticed Joshua Johnson was seven months ago at school (Did the books make me notice? Did my disobedience make me see him?) when I was coming out of quilting bee and headed for home.

"Hey, Kyra," he said as we passed in the hall and he nodded at me like maybe he knew something I didn't.

Oh my goodness, oh my goodness! My heart thumped. His eyes were so blue. Blue like the daytime sky. And he was using his eyes to look at me. Me!

Of course he's using his eyes, I thought and looked at the floor then back at Joshua. "Hey to you, too," I said.

He grinned and I felt my face redden. I hurried out the door and toward home.

Joshua. Joshua Johnson. Blue-eyed Joshua Johnson.

"Oh my gosh," I said just as Laura came running up next to me.

"Where are you off to so fast?" she asked. "And 'oh my gosh' what?"

I swallowed at my jittery feelings, then leaned close to my sister. Her strawberry blond hair was pulled back into long braids. Her eyes, squinty whether she's in bright light or not, looked hard at me.

"You're embarrassed," she said.

Touching my face, I nodded.

"Why?"

"Because," I said, "Joshua Johnson said hello to me."

Laura stopped on the sidewalk that leads from the Fellowship Hall to where we all live. I could see the freckles sprinkled across her nose. "So?"

"So," I said, then I let the words rush out of my mouth. "He is so cute. So *cute*."

Laura stared at me a moment, then started toward home again. "You know you shouldn't even let that thought in your mind."

I said nothing at first, bothered by my sister. She was right. I knew that. But still. "I can look, can't I?"

Laura didn't even glance my way. Just marched toward home. "No," she said. "No, you can't look and you know it."

Again I was quiet, then I said, "You're right, Laura."

She grinned at me, her squinty eyes growing sparkly. "Good then," she said.

But I thought about him anyway. All the way home.

THE LIGHTS ARE ON STILL at the Johnson trailer and so I wait. I wait until all the lights have switched off. I hide near their chicken coop, the smells so thick I could have hurled them at someone.

I hear when the Prophet and Uncle Hyrum walk past.

Hear someone slam a door shut and a coyote cry out and get an answer from someone's dog.

I hear Mother Sarah, and then Father, call me in.

But I don't move. I wait in the dark, the soft cluck of

chickens near, to make sure everyone at the Johnson home is sleeping. Then, in the light of that moon that has turned the color of cream, I tap on his bedroom window.

ONE AFTERNOON, when the sun sat in the sky like a crown on the mountains, I asked Mother if I could go play the piano.

"Just at the Fellowship Hall," I said.

"Of course," she said.

I tucked a fat book of Beethoven under my arm and started away. If I hurried, there would be plenty of time to play. I breathed deep the desert air, happy for the golden light that ended the day. Happy for a moment to fall into my music. I hummed the beginning of a concerto. In my head I could see the notes of a cadenza that was giving me fits. A few minutes of that to start, I decided. Then a jump to the end, maybe fifteen minutes' practice there. That would get my piece . . .

"Hey, Kyra."

I started at the voice. "Aaah!" Then, "What?" And finally, "Sheesh almighty."

Joshua Johnson walked up beside me.

"Oh!" I said, and touched the front of my dress.

"Oh," he said.

30

My face colored.

"That's rude to mimic me like that," I said. I marched forward over the sidewalk, embarrassed. The smell of the desert kicked up from a slight breeze that blew in from the west.

Joshua laughed. "I'm sorry, Kyra," he said, hurrying beside me.

I refused to look at him. Instead, I kept my eyes forward and headed across the parking lot around the Temple, feeling a little angry but more horrified and even more pleased that Joshua had surprised me.

"Where you going?" he asked.

With my head, I gestured at the Fellowship Hall.

"Why? There's no Youth Meeting tonight."

I stopped, planted one hand on my hip the way Mother Claire does when she's especially unhappy, and said, flapping the book at him, "To practice piano, if you must know." *Oh, you are so so so cute,* I thought. *So* cute*! Ahhh!*

Joshua nodded, then shaded his eyes against the setting sun. "Can I come along and listen?"

My heart thumped. He was so pretty to look at, with his brown hair all golden in the setting sun, I didn't know what to do. The only boys I'd been around were my own brothers. And now here was Joshua Johnson.

"What do I care?" I said. But I did care. I did. There was Joshua with those warm-looking eyes of his and that cute face and *Look how tall he is,* I thought, *way taller than me, and he looks so good in that plaid shirt and those blue jeans.*

Don't look at those blue jeans.

You looked at his blue jeans.

I reached for the Fellowship Hall door, but Joshua caught it first and opened it for me. He motioned for me to go ahead.

I did with a flounce, but my foot caught on nothing and I stumbled forward.

Just get to the piano without falling and breaking a bone, I thought. *Just make it to the piano.*

I could hear some boys playing basketball in the gym, could hear the squeak of their tennis shoes on the floor and the echoey pounding of the ball.

"You look pretty today, Kyra," Joshua said. He opened another door for me and we stood in the near darkness of the Assembly Room.

I looked toward the piano. *Just make it there,* I thought. *He is so cute. So cute.*

"Want me to catch the lights?" he said.

"If you'd like," I said. I sat down at the piano, my legs shaking so I wasn't sure I could work the pedals.

The fluorescent lights overhead flickered on and a low buzz filled the room.

Joshua pulled a seat up near the piano bench.

I flipped open Beethoven. Why, I was so nervous my eyes

couldn't make out even one note at first. My fingers trembled and for a moment I wasn't sure if I could even feel them. It was like I was numb. I ran through scales once.

"That was good, Kyra," Joshua said. And then he grinned.

A little laugh slipped from me. "I'm just warming up."

"Play something," he said.

At first my fingers *wouldn't* work. Then, as I played Beethoven, I almost forgot Joshua was sitting right there.

Almost.

Oh, all right. I snuck quick peeks at him the whole time we were together.

And every time, he was looking right back at me.

"You're good," he said when I'd finished my practice. He nodded toward the piano.

"I know it," I said. I wasn't being stuck up. That's a sin, to *think* you're better at something than another person. But the fact is, I *know* I'm better than any of The Chosen Ones so I wasn't being a braggart.

Joshua raised his eyebrows. "And modest," he said.

I shrugged and my brain all on its own thought, *I cannot believe someone like you is talking with me. You smell so good.*

"It takes a lot of work to succeed at this," I said. "A lot of practice. And I want to be good." I waved my hand over the piano, then turned back to the score. Leaning in close to the music, I made marks on the page. Here, here, and here I needed more intensity. Here, I needed less dynamics.

"I want to learn." Joshua stood and moved right next to me. He hit the low E note. The sound thumped in the room.

"Sister Georgia teaches," I said, not even glancing at him, my heart thumping like that low note. "Talk to her. Tell your mother. I'm sure she has time for you."

"My mother?" Joshua asked.

"Of course your mother," I said. I was grinning now. "*And* Sister Georgia."

"But I want to learn from you," Joshua said. He stood behind me now. I could feel his knees in my back. Bony and warm.

Sun broke through the stained-glass window, coloring the air. I could smell the wood oil used to polish the piano. Could hear the boys playing basketball a room over, calling to one another.

His hand rested on my shoulder and my body was flooded with unexpected happiness.

"What?" I should run, run, get away from this sin. Get away. But the bigger part of me wanted to relax into Joshua.

"You're good. You said so yourself. Think you could teach me?"

His hand. His knees. My confused state. I wanted to turn around and hug him. Where were these thoughts coming from?

"Maybe. Maybe, I can." I'm not sure how I got the words out. "I gotta go." I pushed the bench back and struggled to make my legs work. Joshua and I walked across the room. His hands were shoved in his pockets.

"Now, Kyra," he said. We were at the door getting ready to walk into what seemed to me the real world. "What will you charge for lessons?" His face was just a few inches from mine.

I couldn't find my voice. Then I said, "I'm not sure. What do you think is fair?"

Our faces were so close I could feel his breath on my lips.

"I'll figure it out," he said at last.

A CHILLING BREEZE blows across the desert. All around me life has settled in for the night.

I drag an old chair, one I have used at this window, close to the trailer.

I know he sleeps in this room with three other boys. I've never gone to him unless we have planned it first, so he's awake. Usually Joshua comes to my place. Or leaves me a message under a rock in my garden and we meet in the dark near the Temple.

But I have to talk to him. I have to.

"Joshua," I say, whispering through the screen that smells of dust. "Joshua."

My voice is so low, I'm sure he cannot hear it. And I'm shaking. All over shaking. My shin hurts.

"Joshua," I say, his name louder this time and it sounds like thunder. Good grief! Whisper or scream? Choose one, Kyra.

Somebody in the room moves, I can hear them.

"Joshie," someone says. Maybe it's Bryant? The voice is young, not more than two or three. "Joshie, somebody wants you outside." There's a pause and then, "I'm scared."

I should leap down from this chair and take off running, but what worse can happen to me than already has—already will? What can be worse than Uncle Hyrum as my husband? So I wait, still.

"Don't be scared," Joshua says and his voice fills my shaking stomach with relief. "I'm right here."

I squeeze my eyes shut. He's said those very words to me.

THE NEXT DAY AFTER JOSHUA stood so close to me and asked for piano lessons, I found Father. He was coming in from the alfalfa fields, sweaty from the sun and hard work.

"Father," I said before I lost my nerve, "Joshua Johnson wants to learn how to play the piano. May I teach him?" I couldn't quite look my father in the eye. So I stared at the mark his hat left in his hair when he took it off and wiped his face dry.

36

He considered. "Joshua Johnson?" he said. "Where?"

"In the Fellowship Hall. On the old Kawai."

My father, so trusting, who had no idea I had been a moment away from a kiss, nodded and said, "Take Emily with you. Make sure your own music's done. And your chores."

"Yes sir," I said. Had he noticed my pink face? Did he see me blushing?

So I took Emily. She sang the simple notes Joshua played, her voice always right on key. Her voice like a butterfly, fluttering in the air above our heads.

BUT. Here is another secret. Another sin. Because I am not allowed to be with Joshua. I am not allowed to feel this way. Tingly when he looks at me. Weak when his hand is near mine. And the worst part—I couldn't help but wonder how it would be to kiss him.

And when we did kiss, it was all my fault.

Emily in the corner with her baby doll.

Me, in the Fellowship Hall with Joshua.

On the piano bench.

Smelling the soap he uses.

Watching his hands.

Hardly thinking of music.

"This is the chord you *should* be playing," I said to Joshua.

I glanced in his direction and saw him looking at me. Not at the piano keys.

"Put your hand like this," I told him. "You have to look here." I tapped the keyboard.

He let me move his fingers to the right position. So warm, those fingers.

"The C and E and G," I said.

But Joshua's hand didn't stay where I put it. Instead, his fingers tangled up with mine. The whole side of his body leaned into me. His other arm slid around my waist.

"You can't play the piano holding my hand. Or leaning crooked like that, either," I said, my voice breathy. The words almost didn't come out of my mouth. But I thought, *I could kiss you right now and go to hell and it would be worth it.* Worth *it*. I glanced around the room. Emily still played with her baby doll, humming.

"That's okay," Joshua said. "I can wait a minute."

For a long moment we sat together like this. Then Joshua loosened his hand from mine and played the chord like he'd known it all along.

"Good job," I said, his left hand resting on my hip like it was a part of me. My fingertips felt hot, like it was me who'd been playing for hours, not teaching.

"I've been practicing," he said.

"Really? Good," I said. "I'm proud of . . ."

And then I kissed him. Just fell into him right in the middle of a sentence. Pressed my lips to his. So soft. Then he was kissing me back. And I didn't even know *how* to kiss, had never kissed anyone in my life but my family, and then only little pecks on the cheek.

It felt like Joshua sucked the breath from me, there on the piano bench, with all the thoughts of sin going through my head, but me not caring at all. Not at all.

"I better go," I said, when I finally pushed away from him. My hands trembled. My knees shook.

And he said, "Don't be scared, Kyra. I'm right here."

IN THE DARK, I ease around the Johnson trailer. Only the Temple spire is lit up, pointing straight to heaven. Heaven— the place I cannot go now. Not now. Not with all I have done and not with what I'm thinking.

The longer I walk, the longer I try to get away from what has happened tonight, the more I realize that I have to get away. I have to run away.

"You have a month," I say as I walk toward the Temple to wait. "A month to plan. And then go."

ON THE TEMPLE, right over the tall double doors is one large stone eye. It's hand-carved and big as a car.

That eye watches us walk into meetings and out of meetings four hours later. It looks out over the parking lot and the Prophet's and Apostles' homes. It sees the Fellowship Hall and the community building and the cars that come and go. It looks toward the trailers and our gardens and the stand of trees that run back along the river. It watches people shopping in the small store owned and operated by Brother Greer.

That eye sees us all the time.

"God's eye," Prophet Childs says sometimes. "He sees all. He lets me know all."

I used to dream about that eye. In my dream the eye blinked and walked around the Compound looking for something sweet to eat.

There's a concrete stairwell that runs down the rear of the Temple. It leads to a back entrance. The door there's always locked. It's shaded and cool in the heat of the summer. And it's hard to see anyone in that farthest corner, especially at night.

A chain with a sign saying DO NOT ENTER shields the stairwell. No one ever goes there.

Except,

some nights,

Joshua and I meet in that stairwell. We can't talk because

40

our voices echo. But we meet there. I kissed him in that stairwell so long one night, my lips felt bruised the next morning.

JOSHUA'S THERE in just a few minutes. He takes my hands and pulls me to his chest and says, "What, Kyra? What's wrong?"

How does he know I'm scared? Could he hear it when I called his name?

At first I don't think I can even say anything. The words are frozen in my throat. They can't get past my tongue.

"Tell me." His face comes close to mine. I smell his minty toothpaste. He's so warm that the front of me feels sort of calmed down, pressed like I am to Joshua.

At last the words have thawed.

"I've been Chosen."

ONE NIGHT, Joshua and I met near the Temple. No lights burned anywhere because it was after eleven-thirty. Everyone must be in bed by this time. The devil, we've been told, rules the night. Joshua and I shouldn't have been out.

That night I almost laughed thinking about it all. How

we shouldn't be doing any of this. Not touching, not whispering to each other. Not spending time pressed together like we did. *Does Satan rule me?* I wondered. *Rule my body? Is* he *the reason I want to stand so close to Joshua?*

"Kyra," Joshua had said, when he saw me walking to meet him. His voice, low in the dark, headed straight for me and caught me somewhere in the heart.

All the thoughts of what we shouldn't be doing were gone.

We whispered long into the night, sitting in the shadows of the Temple. His arm was around my shoulder. I petted his face like Mother does with Father.

"I saw you today," he said, "walking over to the Fellowship Hall with your music."

In the dark I grinned. "You shouldn't watch me like that," I said.

He stretched his long legs out. Rested his head against mine.

"Tell me," I said. "Tell me when you notice me."

"All the time," Joshua said. His breath was warm in the cool night air. I could hear him smiling.

"Tell me when."

"Okay. Let me think."

I waited, wanting to stay like this forever. I wanted to be like this in the open. In the daytime. In front of others.

"I notice you going into church," Joshua said. "I notice

your hair, how blond it is. But how in some light it looks like it has red in it. I notice the way you smell when we're close. And the way you walk when we're headed home from church and your family gets out of the Temple first. I notice how you are with your family and how you hold your little sisters." He took a breath. "I've seen you stand out on your doorstep and look off across the desert. I've watched you walk toward the Compound fence and then on past that. You've been walking for years."

"You've noticed me for years?" This I can't believe. I'm so pleased with the thought that Joshua noticed me early on, I can hardly stop smiling.

"For a couple of years now, Kyra," he said. "I notice you all the time."

I slung my arms around his neck, kissed his face all over.

"Kyra," he said and his voice was low. "Kyra, I want to Choose you."

"What?" My voice came out high in the night. Too loud for what we were doing. Loud enough to be found out.

"I'm sixteen," he said. "Almost old enough to make a Choice."

I dropped my arms from around his neck. "Well, not for three more years," I said.

"I'm not that far from seventeen," Joshua said. "And two years will go fast after that. I'd work with my father. Raise money. Get us a place of our own." He paused. Took my hands in his. "Would you let me Choose you?"

In that moment a whole line of men, old men, went past in my head. Their mouths in O shapes, their eyes wandering like hands over some of us unmarried girls.

"Would you Choose me, Kyra?" Joshua asked. His face was close to mine, his lips touching my face.

"Yes," I said. "Yes."

NOW JOSHUA HOLDS ME by the shoulders. "What do you mean?" he says.

I tell him everything, everything.

"Your uncle?" he says.

I nod.

"This isn't good," he says after a moment. "He's an Apostle."

We stand quiet, me leaning against Joshua, the two of us swaying.

"I have four Sundays," I say. "Four."

Joshua nods. "I'll think of something," he says.

And I believe him. For the first moment since the Prophet has made his announcement, I feel like maybe, maybe, I have a chance.

IN THE MORNING I am awakened by Mother Sarah throwing up. The walls in this trailer are thin and I can hear her where I lie next to Laura, who snores beside me.

I came in late, late. No one was awake. I found a note from Father on the kitchen table. "I will talk to them, Kyra," it said.

So now there are two people looking after me. Two people that I love.

I crawl out of bed and hurry in to where Mother is. The bathroom smells of vomit.

"Mother?" I reach for her. Her hair, braided long, trails like a snake on the bathroom floor. I can feel the bones of her back.

"Go on to bed, baby," Mother says. Her voice sounds hollow echoing up out of the toilet bowl. She glances at me. Her skin is pale, her eyes watery. She rests her face on the seat.

"Let me help you," I say. My stomach clenches. As many times as I've seen her like this—she gets sick with every baby—it still scares me.

"I'm okay," Mother says.

"Are you done?"

My mother has been sick the whole six months of this, her eighth, pregnancy. Sick enough, I know from library books, she probably should be in the hospital. She's lost three babies already, and very nearly her life besides.

I hook my hands under Mother's arms and try to pull her up. Her belly is the only big thing on her. She sways a little and I try to support her with my body.

"Why, Kyra," Mother says, sounding all surprised. Her breath is awful. "You're as tall as I am. When in the world did that happen?"

If I could smile, I would. But I feel like I have been robbed of everything good. "Mother," I say, "you aren't *that* tall. Laura's creeping up on you, too."

Mother, bent over some, hand resting on her belly, nods.

"Let's get you back to bed. Then I'll make you something light to eat."

Again she nods.

I tuck her into bed, pet her head, then start for the kitchen. I haven't even gotten out of her room when Mother says, "Kyra Leigh. Father and I have talked. He's gone to see the Prophet, early this morning. He'll straighten this all out. I know it."

There are smears of dark blue-gray under both her eyes. I wonder how long it's been since she has slept the night through. Carolina, on a pallet under the window, rolls against the wall.

"I read his note," I say. My heart pounds at her words. At his promise. I might have a chance.

In the kitchen, I start oatmeal and applesauce muffins for my sisters and me, and dry toast with a bit of strawberry jam for Mother. I put water on to boil for her tea. I can hear Laura waking, can hear Carolina talking in her baby voice. Mother answers her. Margaret hums a church song about Jesus being like the morning. Outside the window, it's still dark out.

The smell of cinnamon and sugar fills the kitchen. Water boils.

I stop what I'm doing long enough to hope that maybe Father will save me. I hurry over to his note, fold it, then stick it in my bra so it'll be close to my heart.

I pull my mother's food from under the broiler and spread strawberry jam, jam I helped her make, on the toast.

She's lying in bed, Carolina curled up beside her, talking, talking.

"Thank you, Kyra," she says.

"You're welcome."

"I want something to eat," Carolina says, sitting up.

"Come with me," I say. I put Mother's breakfast on the bedside table.

"I want breakfast in bed, too," Carolina says.

"Do you?" Mother says. She gives Carolina a squeeze. "Then you can stay."

47

"Yippee!" Carolina throws her tiny arms around Mother.

"How about muffins?" I say. "Would you like that, Carolina?"

But what if Father fails? Fear rises in my chest. It races toward my throat.

Stop thinking!

"Yes, yes, yes," Carolina says, her face puffy from sleep.

What if . . . the thoughts might choke me. I think I might die right here in my mother's room. I hurry back to the kitchen.

Mother is so thin. So pale. I love her so much that I can almost not think about it. She's my mother, yes. But she's my friend, too. What will I do when I'm not living with her? What will I do when I have to move out of this trailer to Uncle Hyrum's place? Even leaving my mother, my family, for Joshua would be hard.

But not like this. Not like this.

Fear is like a fist, clutching at my chest. Rising in my body, like it wants to escape from me in a scream.

"Get rid of it," I say.

Laura is in the kitchen now, reading her scriptures at the table. She wears her housecoat, her hair falling loose over her shoulder.

"Get rid of what?" Laura says, looking over at me.

"Nothing," I say. But if I work hard enough, the fear will go away. And if I read. There's a book in my tree.

Harry Potter and the Sorcerer's Stone is wedged in the branches so it won't fall and be discovered. I've read it once, I could start again. Reading would get my mind off things. Or playing piano. Or maybe Joshua.

And I get to go to the Ironton County Mobile Library on Wheels later this afternoon. I can hold on till that. I can.

I dish oatmeal and pull muffins from the oven. The girls and I have prayer, kneeling in Mother's bedroom. Mother prays, asking God to answer the most sincere desire of our hearts.

Is she thinking what I'm thinking? Is she asking God what I'm begging for? Has Father? My other mothers?

Then I sit beside Mother in the bathroom as she throws up her few bites of toast and her tea. The strawberry jam is like hunks of blood. I pray for Mother Sarah. And me.

"REMEMBER," PROPHET CHILDS has said. "God punishes those who sin."

Prophet Childs, as sharp as my Russian Olive thorns, has preached that a woman who dies pregnant or having babies is a sinner. He's said manufactured medicine is from Satan. He's said doctors meddle and take away our God-given freedoms.

Here's what I'd say. Here's what I *know*. If someone,

anyone, would listen to me I would whisper in their ears. I'd say, I know my mother. She's as good as the sun on a cold day. She's sweet to me as honey from the comb. Some nights I crawl in beside her, when Father is with another wife. She always smoothes *my* hair. She always says, "Kyra, you are music to me."

Prophet Childs has said it's wrong to think outside the fences of The Chosen. To think of taking from people outside of our fences.

"We make do with our own and for our own," he's said.

But I have read in the newspapers that the Ironton County Mobile Library on Wheels brings me once a week. I know there is more help for pregnant women. Outside of here. Away from here, there is help.

I HAVE SISTERS and brothers running all over the place. My mother is Father's third wife. Our trailers, one for each Mother with her children, sit in a group, like wagons circling a fire. This is the way it is all over the Compound, not just with us. Fathers with all their wives grouped together. Making a circle. Like how we're one eternal round in heaven.

Sometimes we meet as a family, in the early morning, as

the sun rises, and read scriptures and have prayer, all of us together in that center.

But not this morning. Not this morning because Father has gone to talk to the Prophet in the belly of the Temple, where the Apostles and Prophet meet most mornings before the sun has risen.

Not this morning. While Mother lies in bed, my sisters and I work in the garden. All the homes here in the Compound have huge gardens. They are cut out of the red sand, fueled with manure and rich dirt brought in from the outside by the truckload. Or from the barns where the cows stay the nights. Or from the chicken yards that each trailer has.

It's still early and there is the promise of sun. The sky to the east lightens, and everything around us seems like an old photo, kind of gray. *The way I feel,* I think, *worn out and gray.*

"Jesus loves the little children," Carolina sings, her voice thin and high, just like a baby's. Only all her *l*s make *w* sounds. Her dress is covered with an apron. Her tennis shoes splotchy with dirt. She has a bit of oatmeal on her chin.

Margaret, who is always grumpy in the mornings, stands nearby with the watering can. She has a hand on her slim hip, just like me with Joshua, just like Mother Claire. Margaret's dark hair is loose from last night's sleep. Her lips are a flat line, not a bit of smile coming from her. Her eyes, a fierce brown.

"What's the matter?" Laura asks. But Margaret won't say. For one brief moment I wonder if maybe she knows my sick stomach. Does she realize that I'm leaving home and won't be back? She must. Ten is nearly a woman.

"The morning's grand," Laura says to Margaret.

"Don't be such a sour face," I say.

Margaret looks away. "Your face isn't happy," she says.

I ignore what she's said. I can't even look her in the eye. "Work fast," I say, pulling weeds right next to singing Carolina. "Water please, Margaret."

"You'll leave soon," she says.

I nod.

"Don't talk of that," Laura says to Margaret. Then she smiles at me from where she searches for bugs, squishing them between her fingers. Laura's a lot tougher than I am. "I'm not even worried about this. Father has said he will talk to the Prophet and he will. If anyone can change a person's mind, it's Father."

"You're right," I say. It feels like there's a band around my throat. The band grows tighter and tighter, squeezing my breath away. "Father has gone to the Prophet."

From behind the other two trailers, I can hear my other brothers and sisters working, laughing in the morning, hurrying. A rooster crows, calling to the dawn.

"But he said he had a vision," Margaret says. "Can Father change a vision?"

Laura is quiet.

"Father can do anything," says Carolina.

Now Margaret just waters.

I work, pulling weeds from the damp soil. When the wind is just right I can hear our own chickens clucking, and smell them, too.

Voices call out from the other trailers. I stand, stretching out my back, and listen. There's Adam's voice. And Emily's.

What happened after I left, when everyone went to their own homes? Did Mariah keep screaming? Did they all cry? Did Father comfort them? Or did they say the marriage was a blessing?

Uncle Hyrum. Uncle *Hyrum*.

In the garden I squeeze my eyes shut.

This must be because of my sins. It *must* be.

Carolina stops singing. "Can I water now?" she asks.

I nod. "Of course you can." Quick like, I hug my little sister. Carolina lets me squish her up close for a minute and kiss her. Her face is fat under my lips.

At that moment I see everything, plain. I look at Laura, my very best friend. Look at grumpy Margaret. Feel Carolina close. Her body warm in my arms. The smell of the morning. The sun throwing all those beginning colors into the sky. All of it should save me. All of it should free me of my fears. But instead I have a horrible thought.

I see each of my sisters married to the oldest man in the Compound, Brother Nile Anderson. *Married* to him. He has to be 150 years old. In my head, I can see his spotted hands, yellowed nails, and those fat blue veins that look like they might pop any second.

This comes into my mind because of last night. Of course it does. Because that is what our lives are, I realize, holding on to my little sister.

We are here for the men.

I try to make my mind remember the last time there was a marriage of a young man and a young woman. I can't think of any, not any, not for a long time. It seems all the old men are marrying the young girls.

Like my uncle and me.

It's as though someone punches me in the throat.

Carolina wiggles, pushes away, and starts to water radishes and peppers, sloshing water from the heavy bucket. She's singing again. But Laura, she looks at me.

"What?" she says. "Did a rabbit run across your grave?"

It's something Father says when one of us shivers.

I can't even nod.

"Kyra?" Laura says, and she reaches for me, touches my wrist with her buggy fingers. "What's the matter? Is it last night?"

I shake my head no. I can't say I'm worried for you. I can't say this is all wrong. So instead, I say, "No. It's not last night."

But this little voice of Carolina's? Her little singing voice? It crawls under my skin, burrows toward the gash in my heart. If I didn't know better, I would think for sure I'm bleeding out.

WHEN MOTHER IS ASLEEP, when the gardening is done, I stand on the back porch and look to where I know Amaretto City sits. It's a few hundred miles away, but it's a big place. Big enough for a girl to get lost in.

Marrying Uncle Hyrum is enough to send me away from here.

But if Father can help me . . .
If I ever leave
(should I even think this?
no, I shouldn't even think this)
if I ever leave
(maybe I could)
I'll find me a house
with a piano
and doctors to help
my mother

and no old man
no uncle
to be my husband.

THE THIRD TIME I went to choose a book, the guy in the ball cap said, "Hey, since we're getting to be book friends, I should tell you who I am." He stuck his hand at me. For a moment I didn't even move.

Men and women never shake hands in the Compound.

"I'm Patrick," he said. His hand still out there, like it was hanging in the air. Like it had a mind of its own.

"Okay," I said, reaching forward, just touching his fingers. His hand was cool.

"Patrick," he said. "Just so you know."

I felt glued to where I stood.

"Go on. Look things over," Patrick said, waving his greeting hand. "See what we've got today."

Then he slid around in his seat, watched as I moved in toward the books, slow.

"And my wife's name is Emily," he said, surprising me. "We have one little boy, Nathan."

I hesitated, that day, my mouth full of words. Me, too, I wanted to say. I have those names in *my* family, too. I wanted to say, I'm not the oldest. There's Adam and Nathaniel (like your Nathan) and Finn. I wanted to say I have a sister named Emily—just like your wife. She's older than me. But her mind is slow. I wanted to say all that, but I just kept searching for a book. At last I found *The Borrowers* and checked it out. Then I went to the back of the van and slipped the book into the body of my dress.

"Thank you," I whispered to Patrick, when I came up front with the book good and hidden.

"You bet," he said. "I'll be here next week."

I leapt to the ground, dust puffing up around my feet, and headed toward home.

The engine of the Ironton County Mobile Library on Wheels started behind me.

I moved off the road and, as the van got right next to me, flapped my arms at Patrick.

He slowed the van. Rolled down his window. "Want another book?" he asked.

I shook my head. "I'm Kyra," I said.

"Well, nice to meet you, Kyra," Patrick said and he grinned so big I noticed his front teeth were a little crooked.

I nodded. Stood there.

"Can I give you a lift?"

"No, thank you," I said.

"Then I'll see you next week."

And off he went, with all those books.

LAURA COMES OUT onto the back step with me. She stands beside me, quiet. Neither one of us says a thing for a moment.

Then she reaches for my hand, links her fingers into mine.

Tears spring to my eyes.

"I love you, Kyra," Laura says. Then she leans right into me. I can smell the shampoo we use in her hair. "I love you."

I don't say anything. Just put my face close to hers. Try not to cry. Hold her hand and hope.

I'M MY MOTHER'S FIRST CHILD, born when she was almost fourteen years old.

"Think of it," I said to Laura when I turned twelve. "I'm almost Mother Sarah's age when she was *married*."

Laura looked at me, her squinty eyes even more narrowed. "You could have your own old man as a husband," she said.

"Shut up," I had said.

And she had laughed.

Being the first child is more than just being married early (or first). It means responsibility.

If I were a boy, I'd get to do more stuff, like the boys do here. I could drive any time I was needed (with permission; Mother has taken me out in the family van several times. I'm not too bad considering, though she's said I've given her whiplash.). I could work with the Prophet by carrying messages to families or running errands among him and the Apostles. I could go into town with the others more often. Be a part of the God Squad. Receive revelation for my family.

Choose who I wanted to marry.

MOST DAYS ARE SLOW. With work to fill them up and no time for me to get to the piano or sneak off and read.

But today zooms past. And all I want it to do is slow down. *Give me time here with my family, safe,* I think. *Let my father talk to the Prophet. Let things change for me.*

"Kyra," Mother Sarah says. This afternoon she's not as sick and this gives me more time to worry about what is to come. She sits propped in her bed, spooning chicken broth into her own mouth, and sharing bites with me and Laura and Margaret and Carolina. "Kyra, you're such a good help," she says. "This soup tastes like Mother Claire's home-made."

"I used her recipe," I say. This is almost the truth.

It *is* Mother Claire's recipe, but I stole the soup from her pot yesterday, before all this happened, and replaced it with water. Something like guilt catches in the back of the throat. Is this why I am marrying my uncle? Does the Prophet know that this whole pregnancy I've stolen food from the other mothers so I wouldn't have to make it myself? Does he want to teach me a lesson?

I look away from Mother because I know she never, *never* stole soup from another woman's cooking pot. Especially not as many times as I have.

"Mother," I say, getting ready to tell her everything, like how hard it is to cook dinner for so many. Like how I want to play the piano. Or read. Or see Joshua. But not cook another meal.

She looks at me, her face almost relaxed.

I close my mouth to the confession. She doesn't need this information now. I'll tell her later, when her baby's here, maybe after the blessing. Maybe when I am sick with my own pregnancy. The thought makes my stomach turn over. I don't want anything else to eat.

Carolina bounces on the bed. Her blond hair swings in its braid. Beads of sweat dot her forehead.

"Don't bounce, baby," I say, trying to make my guilt go

away by being especially nice to Mother. "You make Mother's tummy ache."

Our mother nods in thanks. She eats a bit. Shares some more.

Carolina stops her bouncing and says, "Fan Mother harder, Laura. It's hot."

"I'm fanning fast as I can," Laura says. She smiles. I can see she's worried.

All around us, the hot desert air moves from Laura's fanning and the big fan propped in the corner. If we only had air-conditioning like the Prophet and Apostles do, Mother would be able to be pregnant in comfort.

The Prophet.·

Is Father still with him?

Thank goodness there's a swamp cooler plugged into the kitchen window or I swear we'd all go up in a ball of smoke.

"It's hot as hell in here," says Margaret. Then she smiles.

"Margaret," Mother says, her tone disapproving. "Your language is not fitting to that of The Chosen Ones."

Margaret, her face crinkled, keeps smiling. I bet she likes it that she can say a naughty word. "It's straight from the Bible," she says.

Laura fans Mother Sarah harder and says, "Tell us about when you were little."

So our mother tells us about Bible study, when times were easier because sin didn't cover the world the way it does now. When The Chosen Ones were allowed out of the Compound more. How she used to go to the next town and eat Fudgsicles with all her brothers and sisters, before the chain-link fence, before, when Prophet Childs's father was our leader.

We're all quiet, thinking about those Fudgsicles. At least I'm thinking about them. And thinking how Father wasn't so old when Mother married him.

"You were lucky to live then," Margaret says, her voice a sigh almost. "And I'm sorry I said hell." There's that grin again.

Mother eyes Margaret and says, "You're forgiven." Then she breathes out. "I certainly was lucky."

AT LAST I LEAVE the Compound the way I always have, slow like I always do, so no one will think any more of this walk than any other I've taken over the last I don't know how many years.

Are they watching me now that I've been Chosen? Will they follow me?

My whole walk, all the way into the middle of nowhere, I keep checking behind me. I keep looking.

When I can't see the Compound behind me, when I'm sure no one follows, I run, stopping when I grow out of breath. Down the two miles of road, to that dot of trees that makes just about the only shade out here not on Compound property. There's the Ironton County Mobile Library on Wheels.

Parked right there.

"Hey," I say to Patrick when he opens the van doors. He's in his seat, just waiting.

"Good afternoon, Miss Kyra." He nods. Adjusts that ball cap of his.

I want to tell him everything. I want him to know what's happening at home. That I've been Chosen. But I can't. The words get caught right in my throat and refuse to come out. Instead, I plunk down *Harry Potter and the Sorcerer's Stone,* turning it back in.

"I loved it," I say, just getting the words out. "It was great." There's a rock in my throat. When I'm married will I ever be able to come here again? Will I still get books? Still read?

Patrick smiles and says, "My sisters love that book, too. It's a series, you know."

I make my way to the rear of the van and drop to my knees. I can't even look at the titles, I'm so sad. Why did I think coming here would help me? Being here only makes me ache at the thought of never coming back.

"Looking for anything specific?" Patrick says from his seat.

I shrug, not even sure if he's looking at me. "Not really," I say. "Just hoping for something . . ." Just hoping . . . just hoping for what? I don't know why, but somehow, all the sudden, it feels like I could get away in the Ironton County Mobile Library on Wheels.

In a far corner is a rack that has newspapers hanging from it, like quilts made of words. Newspapers from all over the state. And the states surrounding our state and even a New York paper. A New York paper right here.

I've read the newspapers when they have blown free from the garbage pile near the Temple and snagged on the fencing. They're always yellowed and crisp, like the wind and sun has made them tougher.

But here in the Ironton County Mobile Library on Wheels, the newspapers smell of ink. They are new and soft almost.

"We've got company," Patrick says all the sudden.

"What?"

"Hide," he says. "And don't look up. You're not here."

My blood turns cold, makes me feel all watery. How is that possible, to feel frozen *and* as unsteady as water at the same time? I'm not sure I could look out that window if I wanted to.

I slip behind the newspapers. Tuck my dress in close and wait, my heart slamming in my chest so hard I worry maybe whoever is out there might hear.

64

There's a tap on the door. I hear Patrick swing it open, then heavy footsteps. The bus tips a little. Whoever this is, is a big person.

"Need to see your license."

"Yes sir."

Brother Felix! Oh no! I close my eyes, feeling like a baby. Like if I can't see Brother Felix—one of The Chosen *and* our local sheriff *and* a member of the God Squad—Brother Felix might not see me.

There's silence. Blood pounds in my ears. Then,

"What are you doing here?"

"I break here because it's the middle of my day, middle of my route," Patrick says, his voice low and calm. "I rest in the shade of trees."

Again there's quiet. In my mind I can see those eyes of Brother Felix, *Sheriff* Felix, the way he squints and makes you feel like you've done something wrong when you haven't even had the chance. His squinting is not a thing like Mother Sarah's. Not a thing like Laura's. His squinting scares me.

"You might not want to be here too long," he says.

"Won't be," Patrick says. And then, "Am I on private property?"

I keep my eyes closed.

"Close to," Brother Felix says.

There's a pause.

65

"Watch it," Brother Felix says.

"I'll watch it," Patrick says.

The newspaper ink smells so strong I feel sick to my stomach. It's like I have caught Mother's illness, the way I feel weak.

"You come here, you stop here, you don't talk to no one. If I see you talking to someone, I'll arrest you. If it looks like you might talk to someone, I'll arrest you. If I *think* you're talking to someone, I'll arrest you."

"I understand," Patrick says.

If this keeps up much longer, I'll have to figure out how to throw up in my own mouth without making a sound.

Brother Felix moves and the van shifts like we've dropped off a load. The doors shut. There's the sound of a car driving away. I keep still until Patrick says, "You can come out now, Kyra."

My legs won't quite hold me, so I crawl from my hiding place.

"You okay?" Patrick hasn't moved from his seat. He's barely turned around. He catches a glance at my face. "Don't worry, Kyra," he says. "You can keep looking for something to check out."

Maybe I should tell him the truth. That I'm not allowed to read anything but the Bible. Maybe I should tell him that Sheriff Felix and all the God Squad are mean ol' things.

Maybe I should say what kind of trouble we can both get into.

But the books mean too much. There's a chance. There *is* a chance that I'll get back here. And anyway, I *do* have a few more weeks before I'm married. So all I say is, "Thanks, Patrick." And when my legs can hold me, and a good amount of time goes past, I get out of the van, *Anne of Green Gables* hidden in my dress.

"You know, Kyra," Patrick says. He looks at me down the steps. "If you ever need a ride into town, I can give you one."

"Okay," I say after a moment.

Another person who has said he will help me.

I walk away first this time. Go at least a mile. Never look behind me. It's not that long before Patrick and the Ironton County Mobile Library on Wheels drive by. I don't even look at him. Just hope I'll figure this one out.

And remember.

ONE LATE AFTERNOON I read three Dr. Seuss books from the Ironton County Mobile Library on Wheels while sitting on the gritty floor of the van. It's like I'm thirsty and can't get enough to drink.

Early on, Patrick told me I could read if I wanted. He'd stop. Take a break here. Eat a late lunch. Rest in the shade of the trees while I chose something to read.

"Spend fifteen or twenty extra minutes," Patrick had said. "Look around. Enjoy."

And I said, "Okay. Thanks." But I never stay more than ten minutes. A whisper in my head tells me not to. And I trust that voice. Get in, get out, get home and hide the book in my tree if the weather's good.

But this afternoon, I took a few minutes more than usual. I read these books we used to have in our home. Seeing those books makes my stomach feel flat. Seeing these books brought back the memory of smoke. And before that, sitting with Father on the living-room floor, his arms around all us girls, Mother right there, too, reading together.

"I read *Fox in Socks* nearly every night to my boy, Nathan," Patrick said, interrupting my memory. He sipped from a cup that said Big Gulp in white letters.

I pulled *Hop on Pop* from the shelf and remembered Prophet Childs and the Day of Cleansing. This was the first of many cleansings, but of course, I didn't know it then. The memory floods right through me. That smell of smoke.

"Bring your books," Prophet Childs had said.

A fire big as a barn burned in the parking lot of the Temple. I could feel the heat from a distance. Sparks flew in the air and winked out in the night.

"Bring the demon's word here. Burn it all," the Prophet said.

And everyone did. They brought picture books and teen books. Magazines and newspapers. Novels and even the *Reader's Digest.*

"Bring words from the Infidel," Prophet Childs said. "And I will bring you truth. I will lead you to Heaven."

Father and all the mothers from my family brought our stuff, too. Fathers and mothers from other families. Children. Teenagers. Me. We threw the books. The fire ate them up in moments.

Laura was five when this happened. She threw in all her Dr. Seuss books. And cried the whole time. Me, I was dancing and singing with The Chosen Ones, but Laura, she cried.

Seeing her crying, I felt like *I* was doing something wrong.

I went to Laura, took her hand, and held back the worn copy of *Hop on Pop.* I had learned to read from this book. So had she.

"We'll hide this," I said. Smoke filled the air. Cries of joy. The voice of the Prophet.

But Father saw us.

"Burn it," he said.

I held the book behind me. "Let her keep just this one," I said.

Father knelt in front of us. "These are the Devil's words," he said. "You heard what the Prophet said. We must obey."

"Just this one," I said. I put my arms around his neck, whispered in his ear. "Just this one for Laura. She loves it."

I remember I was as hot on the inside as I felt on the outside.

"Just this one," Laura said, draping her arms around Father's neck, too. "Please."

Father hesitated. Then he shook his head.

"Throw it," he said to Laura.

And crying, she did.

"Good for you," Father said. He pulled Laura close. "God will bless you," he said. "God sees what you have done," he said. "I'll let the Prophet know your heart," he said.

Father looked at me. Looked at the fire. He seemed so sad. "Kyra," he said, "you must be obedient."

I remembered all this, the fire hot on my face, the laughter of The Chosen Ones as they danced around the flames, Laura's tears. I remembered all this in the Ironton County Mobile Library on Wheels van and that afternoon I borrowed *Amazing Gracie* from Patrick and left *Fox in Socks* for his little boy Nathan.

WALKING UP TO THE COMPOUND, I see everything in a new way. I've never been truly afraid here, and today, I am. I wonder who knows where I've been. I wonder who knows the pronouncement. I wonder if Father is back.

In slow motion, I walk on toward my home. From outside the fence I can see men working the land. Can see some of the different families' clotheslines, hanging sheets and quilts, dresses and pants, baby things.

The Temple with the Eye watching me, it is a grand building in the light of the afternoon. As I pass through the gates, I see three men in dark suits, even in this heat, sunglasses on as they step from the darkness of the Temple into the afternoon. The God Squad. They're here to protect. The Prophet. Us. The grounds. But seeing them, I'm struck with fear.

"Joshua," I say. I want to run, but I make myself walk in through the gates and on toward home. Like I always do. *Amazing Gracie* sweaty against my belly.

This isn't the first time that the God Squad has seen me coming home. Brother Simmons used to greet me when I was little and sometimes gave me a red licorice when I came back.

He's been gone a long time.

When Mother Sarah was young, there was no problem moving around outside our community. But in the last few years, with a Day of Cleansing that happens every few months, things are different.

I've always walked like this, since I was little, with others

71

walking with me, until a few years ago when I walked alone.

But now.

Now it's dangerous for people to notice.

Joshua has seen me walking toward Patrick and the Ironton County Mobile Library on Wheels, even if he doesn't know that's where I've gone. He's told me he's watched me walking for years.

Does that mean other people have seen, too?

Have they seen me go?

I've been leaving the Compound forever, since I could almost walk.

With Mother Sarah and Father first.

With Emily.

Then with Laura.

Then alone.

Walking past the fence.

Walking down the red dirt road. A washboard road.

Walking to nowhere, then turning around and coming back.

Are they so used to me walking the distance,

outside our fences,

where somehow the air smells different,

are they so used to my walking

that they don't notice anything more?

My heart thumps as I walk past the God Squad. Brother

Adamson nods at me, then turns away. I let out a slow breath of air. Squinch my eyes at the light. Walk when I want to run. First to my tree to hide my book in the leafy branches. And then home.

Where my father waits for me.

II

As soon as I see his face, as soon as I see Mother's face,
I know that Father's request has been denied. They sit together on the sofa. None of my sisters are near. They must
be at another Mother's house.

I fall on my knees at Father's feet. "I can't do it," I say.
"Father, I can't."

He says nothing, just places his hands on my head. He
smooths my hair. I hear my mother begin to cry.

And just like that, there's a knock at the door.

"Please don't make me." I crawl up on the sofa next to

him. He wraps his arms around my shoulders. Kisses my forehead. Mother answers the door.

It's Uncle Hyrum. He is dressed in blue jeans and a long-sleeve shirt. The shirt is buttoned all the way to the top. "Two things," he says before any of us says a word, holding up his fingers to prove it. "I'm here for two things."

I think I've stopped breathing, but I listen.

"Number one. Sister Kyra. I would like to have you over to dinner. A date so we can get to know each other better. Tomorrow evening."

He doesn't even wait for me to answer.

A date?

"And number two, where is the baby from last night?"

Father stands now, loosening his arm from around my shoulders.

"Mariah?" Father says.

"Screaming like that," Uncle Hyrum says. "And in front of the Prophet. It was too much, Richard. Too much."

"She's not even a year old," Mother Sarah says.

Uncle Hyrum looks at my mother like he could slap her. "Don't speak, Sister Sarah, unless I've spoken to you first."

Mother says nothing. Looks away from my uncle.

"Get the baby, Sister Kyra. And her mother. You may leave, Sister Sarah."

"Why?" I say.

He doesn't answer me, but Father says, "Go."

And I go.

Mother Claire, mean as she can be, turns white when I tell her Uncle Hyrum wants Mariah. And her.

"Oh no," she says. "Oh no."

Mariah is asleep on a blanket in the corner, a small fan turned on her.

"She wouldn't stop screaming after you left last night," Mother Sarah says. She bends over, her big belly in her way, and lifts Mariah. "Come here, baby," she says, her voice gentle.

"What do you mean?" I say.

"I just couldn't calm her," Mother Claire says. Her face has gone red now. "No one could. She wanted you."

We leave Mother Claire's trailer. I wish I could feel a bit of pride in Mariah's wanting only me, but this cannot end up good. Not as scared as Mother Claire is.

Mariah has settled back into sleep on her mother's shoulder.

We go into my home, where Father and Uncle Hyrum stand side by side. I'm not sure where Mother Sarah has gone.

"I saw more than I could bear," he tells Father. "More than I can bear," he says to Mother Claire and me and sleeping Mariah.

"She was just tired," Mother Claire says.

"Do not," Uncle Hyrum says in such a loud voice that

Mariah awakens and begins to whimper, "do not speak to me."

Father's hands are clasped and I can see the knuckles are white. Looking at their faces, I can see how these two are related. The same color eyes. The same color hair, same jaw lines. But that is where they change. Uncle Hyrum is a good twenty years older than Father. And a hundred years meaner.

"Strip her down," Uncle Hyrum says. He talks to me. Me! Father stands near his brother.

At first, I think Uncle Hyrum is talking about Mother Claire. Then I see he means baby Mariah. All the sudden I see he's here to teach my father to be a better disciplinarian.

"You're soft, Richard," Uncle Hyrum says right as I realize why he's here. "Soft."

Mariah opens her mouth in a yawn. Rubs at her eyes.

Father says, "Strip her down, Kyra. Do it. Like Hyrum says."

"Father," I say. "Please no."

My father can't look at me. He doesn't spank us, like some of the other fathers do. He seldom raises his voice at us. He hugs us, loves us, laughs with us.

"Kyra," he says after a moment, "please, be obedient. This is an Apostle of the Lord."

I take Mariah from Mother Claire. I take the baby on my hip. She smiles right at me and reaches for my face.

"Water, Claire," Uncle Hyrum says. "And ice."

I take my time removing Mariah's clothes. My heart thumps.

From the kitchen I can hear Mother Claire filling the tin basin first with ice. Then with water.

"Sweet, baby," I say. "Sweet Mariah." I think I'm getting a headache. There's a pain behind my eyes.

Mariah's naked in my arms. She pulls at my bottom lip and lets out a gurgle of a laugh.

"Cover her nakedness, Kyra," Uncle Hyrum says. His Adam's apple bobs up and down. "You know nakedness is an abomination before God."

I wrap the baby the best I can in her clothing.

"Take her to her mother," Uncle Hyrum says.

Mother Claire stands in the doorway now. Water drips from her hands to the linoleum.

I jostle Mariah. "No wait," I say. "Please."

"Take her in to Sister Claire," Uncle Hyrum says.

Mother Claire doesn't move. Neither do I.

"Claire," Father says. I can almost not hear him. It's like his voice and body don't go together. I see his mouth move, but I don't hear hardly anything.

Uncle Hyrum grits his teeth so loud it's like he grinds sand between them.

"She's quiet now," Mother Claire says. "Look how good she is."

"Speak only when I speak to you," Uncle Hyrum says.

Mariah turns to me. Her eyes go squinty with her smile. Her bottom lip is fat and wet. I lean in to kiss her just as she opens her mouth to laugh again. I catch nothing but air.

"Discipline," Uncle Hyrum says to Father, "is God's way to raising righteous children. It's a way you can move up in leadership. I've been telling you this for years, Richard." He shakes his head as if this is the one thing that has kept Father from advancing with The Chosen Ones.

Words jumble in my head. Panic sets in. I can feel it all along my skin, the panic crawling over me. *If I run right now,* I think, holding Mariah close, *maybe, just maybe, I can catch up to Patrick and the Ironton County Mobile Library on Wheels. And he can drive Mariah and me somewhere, anywhere.* The words tumble in my head as I try them out to see if they're possible.

Mother Claire holds her hands out to take the baby. They tremble. She won't look me in the eye. She won't look Father or Uncle Hyrum in the eye either. She cuddles Mariah to her chest. Her belly supports Mariah's bare bottom.

"Deliver the punishment," Uncle Hyrum says. He glances around the room. I don't know what he's looking for. Everyone else has been sent away. But I can see by looking at his face that he's disgusted with my father. His teeth just work. There's that empty space where his tooth should be. Will he

80

end up spitting ground teeth into his hand? "You do it, Kyra," Uncle Hyrum says to me.

I look at Father, my eyes wide. Then I shake my head. "Why me?"

"Just do it," Uncle Hyrum says.

But this, this I will never do. Ever.

"God and our Prophet teach us . . ."

I won't listen.

"Kyra," Father says. He touches my arm. "Your uncle is an Apostle of God."

"I've trained my own," Uncle Hyrum says. "I know the way God directs. You'll do this when you are my wife. You'll do it now."

Mariah laughs at her mother.

"Take the baby, Kyra," Uncle Hyrum says. His voice is sharp as a knife. Filled with anger. But I don't care.

"Administer the punishment," he says.

"I won't," I say.

"No," I say.

"Never," I say.

"Claire," Father says. "You'll have to."

Mother Claire's eyes fill with tears.

"Richard," she says. In all my life, I've never heard her this upset. She's new to me. "Richard."

"Please, Claire," Father says.

Mother Claire covers Mariah's nose and mouth tight so

there's no leak. Then she dunks Mariah in the cold water bath. All the way under. Holds her there.

Holds her there.

Mariah kicks. That baby struggles.

"Stop!" My voice is a shout. I grab at Mother Claire. Father pulls me back.

"Lift her," Uncle Hyrum says. I hate him. Right now, I *hate* him.

Mother Claire has tears on her face. I didn't even know she was crying until she lifts her child.

Mariah's screams shatter the air.

"Again," Uncle Hyrum says.

"No!" Am I the only one alive here? Is it just me and this baby?

"And again," he says.

"Stop it!"

Father holds me with both hands. Keeps me from Mother Claire.

And then, "Enough."

"Control your family, Richard," Uncle Hyrum says. He looks right at me. "All of them." And he leaves without shutting the front door.

"Now, Kyra," Father says. "Dress the baby. Please." His voice shakes.

He and Mother Claire, who's wet all down the front of her dress, stand there quiet. Mother Claire looks at the floor.

Tears drip from her face. Her hands are red from the ice water.

I clutch Mariah to me. Her lips are blue. Her crying is just gasps now. She kicks, trying to catch air.

"Father," I say. "She can't breathe."

I pull her cold body to mine. Slap her little back. She's like a chicken taken from the fridge.

"Father?" It feels like I can't breathe either. I give Mariah a small shake. "Mariah?"

Father steps to me. Pulls Mariah from my hands. Blows in her face. He's lost all color. Mariah's lips are dark blue, like the sky before the sun sets.

"Richard," Mother Claire says. Now her voice is loud. "She's not breathing. Richard!" Her voice rises, goes high. Her eyes are wide. She grabs at Mariah.

Mariah lets loose with a scream so loud I think it might blow out the windows, it might call Uncle Hyrum back.

Father hands the baby to me. He puts his arms around Mother Claire, who sinks against him, and then to the floor. Father pulls her to her feet, then guides her to the sofa in the living room.

It takes me a while to calm Mariah. When her little arms are tight around my neck, I walk her into Mother Sarah and Father's bedroom. I find something warm to wrap her in. A crocheted blanket, all colors of the rainbow.

"If I was going to kill Uncle Hyrum," I whisper onto

her ice-cold face, as she calms in my arms, "I'd do it in Africa."

HOW CAN I EAT with him?
    I hate him. *Hate* him.
    How can I marry him?
    I am sick to the very center.
    I must think of a way out of this.

FOR MORE THAN AN HOUR NOW, I have been in my tree, clutching *Anne of Green Gables*, not even reading it, and hating Uncle Hyrum.

"Kyra." It's Mother Claire calling. Mother Claire, who never talks to me except to tell me what to do, calling me now.

I make my way down out of my tree, careful not to rip my dress on one of the thorns. I make my way to her front steps.

We stand together for a few moments, like we're facing off.

I've crossed my arms across my chest. She's crossed her arms, too.

After she clears her throat, Mother Claire says, "The Prophet tells us be obedient. So do his Apostles. Like it says in the Bible." Her voice is like a reed. Thin and to the point. There is no fear now like there was earlier. Her eyes match the brown of her dress. Her skin is smooth. She's Mother Sarah's older sister. Older by five years. They have the same hair color, the same noses.

I don't say anything, just listen like I care. But I *don't* care. Mother Claire should have run away with Mariah. No, *I* should have. That's what I kept thinking in my tree. I should have run and not looked back. Tied Mariah onto my chest, leapt over the fences, jogged all the way to Florentin, or past that. Out of the state. Away.

"Remember in the Bible where it says it is better to obey than to sacrifice?" Mother Claire says.

I nod. Sort of.

"Kyra." Mother Claire's face is close to mine now. She smells like garlic. I can see she spent some time crying. Her eyes show it. "Listen to me. It's easy to fall astray. It's easy to lose hold of the truth."

When I don't say anything, Mother Clair speaks again. "They watch. They see." Her voice is low as the sand. "They hear what's going on in our homes. They know everything."

Everything.

Fear races up the back of my spine, stopping at my hair.

Do they know Patrick? Do they know the books? Do they know Joshua?

"Your father does what the Prophet says. Screaming babies can mean a disobedient child. We do what they teach us to do. You've heard of people doing what we did today. Others do it more than we have. It's what we're *supposed* to do."

I look Mother Claire right in the eye. Why stay here, I wonder. And she answers with a shrug like she hears my thoughts.

"This is what I know. What your father knows. This is our lives. We are obedient."

It's not my life, I think.

We stare at each other a long time.

Then I nod and go home.

I REMEMBER BEING SIX or seven years old. Father held me on his lap and said, "Always do what God says to do. Always do what Father tells you. And Mother, too."

He caught me outside the Compound fence, just standing there, looking past the chain link. "Kyra," he said at home, me on his lap, "you must be obedient. You must do as you're told. Stay home. Stay close."

"What's out there?" I said.

Father was silent. Then he said, "The world."

"I want to see the world," I said.

"We're safe here," Father had said. "We're away from everyone. Alone. Safe. Out here. Just us. Just The Chosen Ones."

"Looking outside the fence, going outside the fence alone is dangerous," Mother said. "It's like standing too close to the edge of a cliff. You peer over the side, you might fall. You might lose what you have."

But I looked anyway.

THERE'S A NOTE under the garden rock. "Meet me tonight," it says. "Behind the Fellowship Hall. Southwest corner. 1:30."

I can hold on till then.

Mother Victoria comes over after dinner. Father is with her.

"I've settled my brood down," she says, smiling. Her smile is fake. She shows her teeth, and her lips curve, but something is missing in her eyes. Does she know how I feel? Did she feel the same when she had to marry my father? Mother Victoria waves a pad and paper in the air.

"Sarah," she says to Mother, still wearing that smile. "I've come to take measurements."

Laura is in the kitchen, helping me with the dishes.

"Measurements for what?" she says. Even with my hands in hot water I feel cold.

"For Kyra's wedding dress," Mother Victoria says.

"No," I think and until I hear the sound I don't even realize I was going to say this.

Mother Victoria keeps talking, though she stumbles, grasping for words. "Umm. I have some ideas," she says. "You know, to make it, nice."

"No," I say again. My hands become fists. I can smell grease in the dishwater.

"Kyra," Father says and Mother Sarah stands and walks toward me. Laura is silent.

"I won't do it," I say. I drop the dishcloth and turn to face my mothers and my father.

"I've talked to them," Father says. "Kyra, the Prophet Childs says it was direct from God. A vision was opened to him." Father's face has lost color. And he looks old. Old. I'd never noticed before that he's growing old.

"I don't care what was opened to him." I say this between clenched teeth. *Just hold on until this evening,* my mind tells me, *and then you can see Joshua.* "I don't care what he saw." My stomach tumbles on itself. "He wants me to marry my uncle. *Your* brother." I'm almost screaming.

Father flinches.

I run to the bathroom, slipping a little on the wet kitchen floor.

Like Mother, I curl myself around the toilet. I let out a scream, "Aaaah." My voice echoes around my face. Then I throw up so hard it feels like my eyeballs are going to pop out of my head. The skin stretches over my chest, burning. All the day's food, gone. And when I'm sure I'm finished vomiting, when I start to move away, I puke again. Then again. "It's not fair," I say. "I don't love him. I don't even like him." My voice goes high and screechy at the end.

Just hold on.

In another room I hear Carolina say something, then start to cry.

I know I should be quiet. That I should do what I'm told. But I can't help it. Another scream tears from me. Without meaning to, I'm crying.

Someone taps on the door.

"Kyra?" Mother says.

My throat is raw. The room stinks. I've cut the palm of one hand with my nails from making such a tight fist. My nose is stopped up. My heart is broken.

How did I wind up here? How did we all wind up here?

"Kyra?" Mother says. "Father will talk to them again." She doesn't come in the room with me. Her voice is low like maybe she doesn't want my sisters to hear what she says to me. Or maybe she doesn't want those who listen in on us to hear.

It doesn't matter what she says, though. No matter what her promise might be, I can't do it. I cannot bear the thought

89

of marrying my uncle. The thought gives me the dry heaves. Makes my head pound.

I will not do it. I will *not*.

Pushing myself up from the floor, I reach for a towel and wipe my mouth. And right at that moment I decide, without a doubt, no matter what, I'm leaving.

WHY ARE THERE so many babies?

Because children are an heritage of the Lord. Says so right there in the Old Testament. Listen to those words fall from all the Prophets' mouths. Since time began they've been saying this.

During church, when I should have been paying attention and thinking about God, I thought about family. About Joshua and me marrying, having our own babies.

Nothing is like a new baby. Those tight, angry little faces. The way they blink at the light, bothered. Those tiny fists. Squished noses. I love babies fresh from God.

All those babies, coming right here to us.

Coming, maybe, to Joshua and me.

If.

UNCLE HYRUM SHOWS up for dinner, and us not even expecting him.

He makes Father leave Mother Victoria, though this is Father's week with her. He makes Father come to dinner at my house.

"We need a man to chaperone," he says, "to show that I'm honorable," and he claps Father on the back with a laugh. Not one of us laughs with Uncle Hyrum. He settles on the sofa.

"It's good to see the women of the community," Uncle Hyrum says, "to see how they run their homes."

Mother glances over her shoulder at him. I know she wasn't planning a big dinner, nothing more than pancakes. She scurries around the kitchen, then says, "Come with me, Laura. And Kyra, please set the table." The two of them hurry out the back door. Mother doesn't look like she feels that great again. Maybe Uncle Hyrum has made her sick to her stomach. He sure has me. I try not to look at him while I work. But I can't help it. I steal glances at him and Father as they sit in the living room.

His hair is gray at the temples and is slicked back with something that makes it appear wet. His shirt is buttoned all the way to his throat again.

Carolina sneaks over to Father's lap. He wraps his arms around her tight.

After a few moments, Mother comes back into the house.

She carries a platter of roasted meat with carrots and potatoes lining the plate. Laura has a pan of rolls in one hand and a pie in the other. I'm betting they've been to Mother Claire's house. We haven't eaten this good for months because cooking meat makes Mother want to puke. I can't believe how good the food smells.

My mother says, "We're ready, Richard."

Father nods and he and my uncle come in to sit at the table.

Uncle Hyrum presides, taking Father's chair. He makes me sit next to him. And makes Mother Sarah eat with us, too, though her lips go pale as she sits there. I'm not sure if it's the beef or Uncle Hyrum that make her feel sick.

"Dear God in Heaven," Uncle Hyrum prays when we kneel at our chairs for the blessing on the food. "We thank thee for this bounty. We thank thee for the truth. Help us to see it and be believing. Help those here who must yield."

I think my heart might stop beating. If I'm lucky, my heart *will* stop beating. But there is Joshua tonight. I can make it till one in the morning. I could do anything until one in the morning.

We wait for Uncle Hyrum to fill his plate. I make sure there's grape juice in his glass at all times, like he tells me.

Uncle Hyrum has six wives of his own. Six! What does he need one more for? Why? He's greedy.

I can tell by the way he eats. With his mouth open. And

piling so much on his plate there's hardly any left for the rest of us.

No one speaks but Uncle Hyrum. He talks on and on of God and his family and the blessings that are his. The blessings that will soon be mine.

"Just one month," Uncle Hyrum says, "and you, Sister Kyra, will be bound to me and headed toward heaven."

What can I say to that? Nothing.

What do I think? *You make me sick. With your balding head and meat stuck in your teeth and the way you smack your lips when you eat. You make me sick and I'm not planning on sticking around here. I'll leave, I'll take my sisters away, I'll go. You can't make me stay here.*

He smiles and I see where his tooth should be and I realize this is another reason to hate him.

He talks and talks. About discipline. About obedience. About lalalalala and dadadida. If I could get to a piano right now, I would play Chopin. I would try a bit of Liszt. I would hammer out Beethoven just to make this uncle—my future husband—be quiet. I could care less that he's an Apostle. I just want him to shut up. How could this man be my father's brother?

At last, at last, Uncle Hyrum is done eating. He calls on Father to say the closing prayer. My uncle hasn't spoken to anyone once. Just at us. He's never asked for a response. And all I can think is how much I hate him.

Then Uncle Hyrum says, "Kyra, walk me to your gate."

"We don't have a gate," I say. Bricks line our yard, separating it from my father's other wives' yards.

"Oh yes," he says. His eyes are like buttons. The kind on an old coat that have lost their shine from so much use. I hate him! Hate him and his button eyes.

I keep sitting.

"Kyra," Father says, his voice low coming across the table at me. Margaret says, "Don't make her go with him." She starts to cry and then Carolina bursts into tears, too. Laura hurries to the kitchen sink like she's anxious to do the dishes. Now I feel like I might weep, but I don't. I feel so much hate, I could spit.

I walk to the door where Uncle Hyrum stands. He tries to take my hand in his, but I won't let him.

I'll never let him, a voice that I don't even recognize screams in my head.

Outside the evening is cool and the moon has given the yard a milk-washed look.

"Do you understand what is about to happen?" Uncle Hyrum says when we reach the bricks that border my mother's yard. He doesn't wait for an answer. "I don't think you do." He links his hands behind his back and rocks on his heels. He stares off toward the Temple. "You were saved for me. I saw you when you were young and prayed for you to be mine then." He's quiet a moment. "Doing what you're supposed to do will make life much easier for you, Kyra. And your father. And your mothers." He takes a breath. "Don't send your father to Prophet Childs again."

My backbone straightens and I look right at Uncle Hyrum's face. I think, *I'll ask Father to go again and again and again to see the Prophet.* I think, *I'll ask him until Prophet Childs and God hears me.* Uncle Hyrum doesn't look at me. Just keeps staring away.

"You know what happens to those who contradict God, don't you?"

I try not to, but I gasp.

Now Uncle Hyrum looks at me and smiles. He's won and he knows it. "God has given you to me, Kyra Leigh. You *will* do what He says. What the Prophet says. What *I* say." Then Uncle Hyrum walks away and leaves me standing in the milky night.

I REMEMBER BILL TROPHY. He was *always* laughing. Throwing back his head and laughing so that I was surprised at the large sound of it. Mother said he had a great smile.

"But," she whispered to me and my sisters when Father wasn't home, "he should have listened to the Prophet."

Bill went missing three or four years ago. I bet he wasn't even eighteen when he ran.

I remember.

"He's with the Lost Boys," Mother said. "Gone off with them. That's where all those boys end up. Somehow they end up together." Mother looked away. "That's what we've heard. That's what we hope."

And Ellen. Quiet Ellen. Opposite of Bill. Mother said she was delicate of bone. Tiny.

I remember Ellen and Bill together.

I remember Mother Sarah telling me to always be obedient.

I remember shots ringing out.

And I wonder why Bill Trophy was allowed to run to the Lost Boys. And not Ellen.

Ellen chose Bill. (You never get to choose if you're a girl.) That loud laugh of his.

Ellen chose Bill Trophy.

Remember?

I remember.

I walk inside, shivers covering the whole of me. My brain running a million miles an hour.

Bill ran.

Mother and Father stand in the kitchen. His arms are around her and she rests against him.

Look what I have caused, I think. *Look at their grief.*

"Come here, Kyra," Mother says. She opens her arm to

me and when I get close to them, both she and Father pull me in tight.

I am face-to-face with Mother. Her eyes are filled with tears. I can't even look at her she's so sad. Her face shows how I feel.

Father kisses both of us on the tops of our heads. He holds us secure. But his holding me like this is a lie. He can't do anything to save me. And he's my father.

Aren't fathers supposed to save their daughters?

We stand like this, the three of us, for several minutes. Then Father says, "I have to go."

He leaves Mother and me standing arm in arm.

I am tired from the inside out. I am so tired at that moment it feels like I could melt away with no problem. If only.

I walk Mother into her room. I want her to tuck *me* in tonight, have her check under my bed for monsters, have her pat down my blankets, fluff my pillow. But I saw her face at the dinner table. She looks to be on the edge, too. I sit on her bed.

"Tell me about Bill and Ellen," I say.

Mother doesn't say anything at first, then, "You remember them?"

I shrug. Only a little light comes in from her window. We are shadows in her room, so I'm not sure she sees me.

There's the scent of lavender in here. Lavender meant to settle Mother's stomach. "They just came to me," I say.

Again, Mother is quiet. "She was an example," she says.

I nod. The air is still and hot. Heavy. Like a blanket.

"Sister Ellen married Brother Mathias," Mother says.

I had forgotten *that* part. There was a wedding.

Lots of girls getting married. Maybe thirteen or fourteen different girls being married to several men. Including Ellen, one of Brother Bennion's daughters, who had to marry Brother Mathias, an Apostle. He was at least seventy years old then. His teeth, yellow. His eyes, too. Like an egg almost. He sat at the front of the Temple during meetings, with all the leaders up there in white suits, looking us over.

At the ceremony Ellen cried. Oh, she cried. Wailed. Fought. Screamed for her mother to help her. Screamed for her father to save her.

"She's crying," I had said to Mother. Fear raced through me, watching this.

"Hush," Mother said, squeezing my hand.

"She doesn't want to get married," I said to Laura.

Laura looked at me, her mouth a small O. Her squinty eyes wide.

The Prophet spoke louder.

And it was Sheriff Felix who quieted Ellen with a hard slap to the face so the ceremony could go on.

"Then what?" I say.

98

"She saw someone else," Mother says. Her voice drops to a whisper even though we're alone. "She loved someone else."

"What do you mean?" I say. I think of Joshua. Oh Joshua.

"Intercourse," she says. "Adultery." And it's like she's shouted the words in this small, quiet room. Beside us, on her pallet, Carolina turns and mumbles something. "With Bill Trophy."

Mother Sarah takes in a breath. "She was my cousin." She whispers still.

"Bill was Ellen's age. Maybe a year older. They sent him away. No one knew what happened. He was just gone."

The room is so quiet now I hear myself swallow.

"What happened to her? What happened to Ellen?" I say. "Did they send her away, too?"

In the next room someone rolls over and kicks the wall. The sound startles me and I jump.

"What happened to Ellen?" I ask again.

"They killed her," Mother says.

I REMEMBER! I remember!

The sound of the gun going off.

Mother and Father and the other mothers talking about

99

it afterward. In hushed voices. Telling us in whispers at family time we must be obedient and love God.

Father crying. Looking at all of his children and crying. Those great big family meetings, all of us together, Father's wives and children, all my brothers and sisters. Me hugging his neck. Afraid and not sure why.

And Father holding me on his lap, his arms tight with his grief.

THE WHOLE HOUSE IS QUIET when I leave to meet Joshua.

Not a sound as I tiptoe from my shared bed, into the living room, and then out the door.

Once outside, I breathe free. I whisper, "I'd have left Brother Mathias, too."

I trudge past where Father and Mother Claire sleep and little Mariah, past Mother Victoria's trailer. I head toward the Temple, the steeple guiding me. I hurry toward Joshua, the awful memory of what happened to Ellen, all because she loved someone else, fat in my head.

JOSHUA'S THERE! Waiting. I know it before I even see him. And when I get close to the darkness the building and night makes, his arms reach out for me and pull me in.

"Kyra," he says. "Kyra."

Right when he pulls me near, I know why Ellen chose Bill. She must have felt this way.

"I can't do it," I say and start crying. Still, tears and all, I kiss Joshua.

"Wait," he says. "I want to tell you something."

But I won't let him speak. "This might be my last time with you," I say. And I'm kissing him again, my arms wrapped around his neck, my hands in his hair, my body pressing as close to him as I can.

Joshua touches my face, gentle. He starts talking, all the while I'm kissing his lips and cheeks and chin and neck.

"Kyra," he says, almost laughing, his voice low in the darkness. "Listen. I have to say something important."

"Okay," I say. Something desperate fills me. Fear? Pain at remembering Ellen? Worry that Joshua will tell me we must do as the Prophet has said? I close my eyes, resting my forehead on Joshua's chest.

He holds me by the shoulders. "I've made an appointment to meet with Prophet Childs. To speak to him about us. To tell him I want to Choose you. That I want to marry you."

I open my mouth to speak but Joshua keeps talking.

"I've been praying about it," he says, "and I think we should be together." He pauses. "If you'll have me, Kyra." Again he pauses. A breeze sweeps in from the desert, cool and smelling of sage. "Will you have me as your husband?"

I'm not sure when Joshua became *my* Joshua. I'm not sure when I first kissed his eyelids. I'm not sure when I first moved his hair from his forehead.

This I am sure about. In my heart, I claim him.

A WHILE BACK I told Joshua about the Ironton County Mobile Library on Wheels, about my choosing books and bringing them to the Compound. It took all my courage. All my hope that he wouldn't think I was crazy stupid for doing such a crazy stupid thing.

"Look what I have," I said that night we met.

The evening was light with a full moon the color of butter. I held the book out to Joshua before I even hugged him.

He took it from my hand. "*Homecoming?*" he said. He was quiet, looking at the title like he didn't get what he saw.

My heart sat in my throat, nearly kept me from breathing.

"Kyra," he said, looking at me in the moonlight. "Do

you know what this is?" For a moment I felt like Eve giving Adam the apple. Would Joshua bite?

I nodded, my braid feeling extra tight, tears stinging at my eyes. If he wanted, Joshua might stop seeing me because of this. But I had to show him. *Had* to let him see this part of me.

He lowered his voice, talking as though I wasn't there. "Books aren't allowed. Where did you get this?" His hand smoothed across the cover.

"Our kissing isn't allowed," I said. "Our secret meetings aren't allowed. Me being with you tonight isn't allowed."

He said nothing. Opened the novel. Leafed through the pages.

"Do you miss reading?" I stood back from him, the book between us.

"We read," he said, but he didn't look at me, just at *Homecoming*.

"Don't you miss *novels*?" I said. "Don't you miss fiction?"

It was a long moment. Long enough that worry grew in my stomach. By showing him this book I'd given Joshua something I couldn't take back. I'd handed him a bit of my freedom.

"Never mind," I said, tears threatening. I reached for the novel, tried to take it from him, but he wouldn't give it up. Instead, Joshua opened the cover again, touched the pages, lifted it to his nose. His voice came out low. "My mother used to read to us, all of us gathered around her on the sofa, me and my younger brother on her lap."

I was quiet then I whispered, "Me too."

That night, hidden in the darkness of a building, but holding the book so we could see the words, we read the first four chapters of *Homecoming* together, our voices light as the breeze in the desert air.

IN THE MORNING Father comes to our home with Mother Claire and Mother Victoria. He announces that the mothers will take me to town for material.

"What for?" I ask. I'm still a little asleep though I've had breakfast and done family scripture study with my mother and sisters. I can't help but wonder if any of the kisses I shared with Joshua the night before are obvious. Are my lips marked? The skin of my face?

"You've got business in town," Father says. He doesn't quite look at me. "Your mothers will help you."

I never go to town. Haven't been in I-don't-know how long. Men and boys go to town. Women and girls and babies stay here, where they will be safe.

Safe! Ha!

"What do we need material for?" I say. I think of the

quilt I started so long ago and that I haven't sewn a stitch on. I don't love to sew.

Mother Claire is all business, brushing her hands together though I can't imagine there's anything to sweep away. "For a wedding dress," she says, her words clipped short.

Mother Victoria stares out the window. My own mother dips her head, avoiding my eyes. Father clears his throat and says, "I'll have the older children take care of the younger while you are gone." Then he leaves the room, fast.

A wedding dress? At first I can't find my tongue. When I do I say, "I don't want a wedding dress." My voice is loud.

Margaret comes from the bathroom and stands beside me. "She doesn't want a wedding dress," she says, "and I don't think you should make her get one." She speaks to the living room full of mothers. There's an awkward silence. Everyone is still. I don't think I've ever heard Margaret sound like this.

"Go clean the dishes," Mother Sarah says to Margaret. The room snaps back to life. "Go right now, young lady."

Margaret hesitates.

"Kyra, you be ready to leave in thirty minutes," Mother Claire says. "I haven't got all day. And neither do you."

Mother Sarah reaches for my hands. "It'll be fun," she says. Her face looks plastic, her smile forced.

"She doesn't want to get married," Margaret says. She

touches my back, her hand small. Mother ignores her, something she doesn't do often to any of us.

"We'll go to lunch," Mother Victoria says. "The fabric store first. And then lunch at Applebee's. I haven't been there in a year. How does that sound?"

For a moment it seems like these women are chickens, like I've read in my books. They're busy and in my face and commanding. And if we were headed to town for something I wanted to do, this would be fun. Lunch out? I've never had food anywhere except here, in the Compound, fixed by one of my mothers or by other women when we have holiday celebrations.

"A fresh dress, Kyra," Mother says. She points toward my room.

Margaret stands beside me, little and unhappy.

The three mothers go their separate ways but not before Mother Claire says, "We have to have her home in time for dinner with Brother Hyrum. We'll have to hurry."

Oh, the date tonight. That *date*. Wasn't last night enough? Fear and anger, both, seem to fill me.

"Hell," Margaret says. "Helly hell hell." Then she throws her arms around my neck in a tight squeeze. I can smell her face, sort of sweet like sugar. Then she hurries into the kitchen to wash the dishes left over from breakfast and I keep standing where everyone has left me.

If I were allowed to love Joshua, I would tell them all

106

right this *very* second that yes indeedy I *could* use wedding dress fabric because Joshua was speaking to the Prophet on this *very* day about me marrying *him*. But I can't say anything. So I stomp into my bedroom and grab a different dress and a fresh pair of tights. My eyes are filled with angry tears.

"Kyra?"

Laura stands in the doorway. I can hear water running in the kitchen. Somewhere Carolina is playing.

"Mother said I could go with you," she says. She wears a dark blue dress and her eyes remind me of a picture of an ocean I saw in a book in the Ironton County Mobile Library on Wheels. "If you want."

"I do," I say. "I want you to go, Laura."

"ARE YOU READY, Kyra?" Mother Claire stands looking into my room with Mariah on her hip. "We've got a long way to go."

I've washed my face, changed my clothes. I feel like Laura in a *Little House on the Prairie* book. The way they got dressed up before heading to town so they would be respectable.

My Laura and I have braided each other's hair. We've made sure our dresses are ironed, that our white tights have no holes. I've polished our black shoes.

Neither one of us speaks. There's nothing I can do to change this. Nothing. I grab Laura's hand.

Outside, it is a lie of a morning. Everything is beautiful: The air fresh. The sky so blue it hurts my eyes. A breeze moves my Russian Olive trees. It's like they are waving me a good-bye. All is quiet except for the cry of a baby from someone's trailer.

Mother Victoria jangles the keys. "Let's go," she says, grinning. She seems anxious to get away. To travel out of here and into the real world.

We head to the family van, a sixteen-passenger that we outgrew years ago.

Mother Sarah sits shotgun. Mother Victoria starts the engine while Mother Claire fastens Mariah into her car seat.

I slide in on the middle bench and pull Laura with me.

We drive forward, moving slow through the black-topped streets, past the trailers, the Temple, the store, the Fellowship Hall. We're headed to the gates of The Chosen Ones.

When people go to town, they go in groups of three or four families. "There is safety in numbers," Prophet Childs always tells us.

But not us. Not today. It's just my three mothers and Laura and baby Mariah, because she's so young.

I glance at Laura sitting there beside me, quiet.

Could I live without any of my sisters? Without Laura? Even for Joshua?

Laura squeezes my hand but doesn't look at me.

Even in my imagination, could I leave her?

But I *am* going to leave her.

In one month, I'm gone.

The fabric, this morning.

The date, tonight.

All the days will fly past.

And then I'll leave these women and my sisters and brothers and my father and go to live with my uncle. The thought causes real pain right in the center of my chest.

Mother Victoria turns left toward town—fifty minutes away—the opposite direction I go when I walk to the Ironton County Mobile Library on Wheels.

My mothers, all of them, once we are free from the Compound, start to talk. They laugh with each other. They tease. They tell stories about "before," when they traveled to town anytime anyone wanted.

Down the rutted road toward civilization we all go, me listening to their laughter, headed to the things that will help me start a new life I do not want.

I will be a seventh wife.

ONCE, A FEW YEARS BACK, I saw Mother Sarah angry at Mother Victoria.

I listened in at the back door that stood open to let the morning's cool air into the trailer. I peered in the window. I saw the whole thing. Laura and I were supposed to be pulling bugs off the watermelon plants. But I heard Mother's voice coming out the kitchen window.

"Just because I'm younger, she's angry with me," Mother had said.

There was something in her voice that made me want to eavesdrop. I crept under the window to listen.

"What are you doing, Kyra?" Laura said, looking over and seeing me. Her arms were crossed. "You have to help."

I held a finger to my lips. "I will," I said. "Just give me a minute."

"It's jealousy," Mother Claire said. "None of us can help but feel it. Sharing a man the way we do."

"She gets nasty sometimes," Mother Sarah said.

"You're supposed to be working," Laura said.

I waved at her like I was flapping away flies. "Shhh," I said. But I thought, Sharing a man? What did *that* mean? Like I shared work with Laura? Or toys with little Margaret?

There was quiet in the trailer for a minute. Then Mother Claire said, "Follow the Prophet, Sarah. We give up things now for a life in the hereafter that will be better."

"I know," my mother said. Her voice was soft with tears. "But, I'll never be a first wife. I'll never be anything but a third wife to him."

110

WHEN DID MOTHER SARAH get over being unhappy? And how long did it last? And would she have felt this jealousy if Father had been an old man like Uncle Hyrum?

"IS THIRD BEST?" I asked Mother Sarah, later, much later. I remember Father was gone to another wife's house, but I'm not sure which one.

"What do you mean?" Mother asked. It was bedtime and my younger sisters were all asleep themselves or getting ready for bed. Mother slipped from her dress into a nightgown that hung all the way to the floor.

"You're the third wife," I said. I looked off over the bed toward the window. Joshua and I had just started meeting in secret. Could I share him? I wondered. "Do you feel, like, third place?"

"Oh," she said, surprise in her voice.

Out of the corner of my eye I watched her pull her hair free from its braid. Her hair so long she can sit on it. And thick, too. Beautiful to run your hands through. I have, brushing it till it shines in the bulb light of this room.

Did Father do that?

I was embarrassed by the thought.

"Are you ever jealous?" I wanted to say "still." Are you still jealous? But I didn't.

My question hung in the air. Mother walked through it to climb into bed.

"This is God's way, Kyra," Mother said after a long while. "This is God's choice for us. Prophet Childs has told us so."

But what do you *think?* I wanted to ask her. I didn't. Instead, I just ran a brush through Mother's hair for her, feeling the heavy silkiness of it and smelling the odor of lavender.

One day, I thought, *I'll leave home. Start my* own *family.*

I was struck with how I would miss this. Miss my mother. My sisters. My throat tightened and I thought I might choke. Oh!

Tears rolled down my cheeks. Dripped from my chin. But I kept brushing my mother's hair, until she was ready to sleep.

I'VE SEEN WOMEN screaming at each other. Fighting over their husband. It's true. Not often. But once it happened right outside the Temple. Three women married to

Brother Smythe. He stood there between them, trying to keep one wife from hitting another.

The Prophet was called. And all us kids standing around watching things unfold were sent home.

"This is the Devil's work," Prophet Childs said. "Get on home to your fathers and tell them what you saw."

We ran.

Father told us all that evening those three women were beaten by the God Squad.

"They'll not step out of line again," Mother Victoria said. Her lips were thin and white.

Mother Claire just glared. Making sure we each saw that she disapproved what those wives had done, I guess.

"Next time," Mother Sarah said, "you come home when something like that starts to happen."

"I will," I said.

But I couldn't help but wonder about the little red-headed wife. Not more than fifteen. Maybe. Those other two women pulling on her, slapping at her. Because she was prettiest, I bet. And thin still. Not chubby like the others, though I could see the shape of her belly growing under the dark green of her dress.

MOTHER VICTORIA DRIVES GREAT. She flies along the two-lane road like she is a professional driver. Uses only one hand on the steering wheel, even. Better than Mother Sarah when she taught me.

"We have an engagement to attend to," she says, eyeing me and Laura in the rearview mirror. She can't wait to get to Applebee's. Every once in a while she laughs with happiness, just from being out from the Compound, I think. Her laughter causes us all to smile.

"You're dead crazy," Mother Claire says.

I watch as the world zips past. Look at the sky. Sit quiet next to Laura.

I want to tell Mother Victoria to slow down some, so I can see everything.

If I run away, this is the direction I'll go. Florentin is north of here a few hundred miles. That's what the map in the Ironton County Mobile Library on Wheels says.

Soon the barren land grows greener. There are more houses. Then more cars. Just like that, Mother Victoria loses her professional-quality driving. She puts her foot on the brake so often I think I might get whiplash. She drives close to other vehicles—not just too close to cars, but to buses and trucks, too. It's scary. Mother Sarah is white-knuckled in the front. I can see her hand gripping the armrest.

Mother Claire gives instruction from her seat right behind Mother Victoria. "Watch it on your left," she says.

"Brake! Brake! Brake!" And "If I get out of here alive, Victoria, I swear . . ."

"Stop it, Claire," Mother Victoria says. She's leaned forward, her face almost over the steering wheel. "You keep startling me."

"I can't look," my mother says, covering her eyes.

From the middle seat, Laura and I stare out the side window. There are people everywhere. Cars everywhere. Horns blare. Stores and car lots and restaurants line the streets.

If I have ever thought of running away—well, seeing all this slows me down some. How could I manage to get around in this? And surely Florentin would be much worse.

But, a voice says in my head, *if there's enough people* they *couldn't find you, you'd be safe*. I push the thought away.

Laura has moved behind me so she can get a better look out the window. "There has to be a million people here," she says. "Look at them all. And look what they're wearing."

"Do *not* look at their clothes," Mother Claire says. She pats Mariah's cheek and doesn't even glance at the people outside. "They're from Satan." The baby is getting fussy. Not used to being strapped down for so long. Or maybe she's worried about Satan, too. Ha!

Mother Sarah rolls down the windows. Dirty-smelling air comes in our van. I keep staring at people wearing Satan clothes. What I see are girls in blue jeans, and guys, too.

Every once in a while, some man or boy doesn't have his shirt on.

We maneuver down the street. People seem to be beeping at *us,* maybe because we're going so slow.

"Keep a steady pace, Victoria," Mother Claire says. "We've got to be almost there."

My mother laughs a nervous laugh. I can see her profile. She looks kind of gray near her mouth. This back-and-forthing must be making her sick to her stomach.

Laura looks nervous, too. "I'm scared," she says where only I can hear. "All these people."

I nod.

"There! There it is," Mother says. She points a shaking finger to a line of stores across the road.

"Oh no," I say to Laura. "Close your eyes. She's got to cross all that traffic."

We make it to the parking lot of where Carole's Fabric Store is, with only one man in a truck having to screech on his brakes. He lays on the horn, beeping all the way past us and then some.

"We're alive," Laura says when the van stops. She grins full in my face.

I grin back.

Mother Claire unbuckles Mariah from her car seat. Laura and I climb out and into the parking lot. The world smells like hot tar right here.

"Don't say anything to anyone," Mother says as she gets out. She slams the door shut. It feels good not to be rattling around still. I'm glad to be on solid ground.

"They'll look at us," Mother Claire says. "They'll stare. But you ignore them, girls. You remember who you are. The Chosen."

"Yes, ma'am," Laura and I say together. We follow our mothers down the sidewalk. The air is hot. The sun beats down. It must be noon straight up.

A family leaves the grocery store. The boy pushes the cart ahead, jumps on it. Rides to the parking lot, passing us.

His mother sees us and calls, "Ryan. Wait for me. Wait for me right there." She casts a glance at us as she goes by, a little red-headed girl in tow.

A brown-haired girl with a several streaks of pink color rushes toward the grocery store, tying on a red apron. She takes a moment to stare at me and Laura, then runs on inside.

I grab hold of Laura's hand, squeeze it. Ahead is a group of girls just older than me.

"Let's go, Kyra, Laura," Mother Claire says over her shoulder. She's gotten to the fabric store door. She turns and waves, like she's trying to hurry us. Her face has two bright splotches of pink in it.

The girls break apart like the Red Sea must have for Moses and let us pass. We haven't even gotten through the six or seven of them, when one throws back her head and laughs.

"Freaks," a girl says.

As we pass the glass window of the shops, I catch a glimpse of us in the storefront windows. Laura and me in long dresses, our hair pulled back, our arms and legs covered from sight.

I see plain as day we don't look like anyone else in this town. The girls here wear blue jeans, T-shirts that show their bellies. One girl, who leans against the brick of the fabric storefront and smokes (smokes!) a cigarette, has an earring in her eyebrow (her eyebrow!). There's a dragon (a dragon!) on her arm. Long, curled down and around her arm, its tail touching her elbow. She looks at me, her mouth hanging open.

I can't stop myself. "What are *you* staring at?"

Then I slip into the Carole's Fabric Store before Dragon Girl can answer. The door lets out a tinkling sound. My mothers have moved ahead of us. Laura drags me along. For a moment, I can't see, that's how angry I am. I squeeze my eyes shut, then open them again. There is so much fabric in here, so many colors, that I am reminded of the dragon on the girl's arm. Lots of colors there, too.

The whole world is different than we are, I think. The whole wide world.

And I'm horrified. Embarrassed. I feel everyone's eyes on

us. Even here in the coolness of the store, people notice. They are *watching*. I see it. I hurry to where our mothers are, near bolts of flannel. I hear people whispering.

"Polygamists," someone says, "you can tell by their clothes."

If I hadn't found the Ironton County Mobile Library on Wheels, if I hadn't found words, if I hadn't found out that I love Joshua, would I feel this way today? So much has changed in me because of a few things. How can that be?

"Oh, Kyra," Laura says. Her cheeks are stained red. Tears have filled her eyes. She stands behind Mother Claire, then takes Mariah, who reaches for me when I get near. Outside, a car horn goes off again and again. This place is crazy!

"Did you see that girl?" I say. My back is straight with anger.

Laura says nothing, just looks at the tile floor.

"She was outside."

My sister kisses the baby's face.

I look through the huge glass window. There she is. Dragon Girl, cigarette still in hand, works to unlock her car door. The beeping continues.

"Her," I say, pointing.

Laura looks, then shakes her head. Tears run down her face. She turns her back to me.

Now I am really mad. Make my sister cry? My Laura

cry. There's a part of me that wants to run out to Dragon Girl. Grab her by her black hair. Throw her on the ground and punch her face in.

But what about everyone else? Would I have to smack the cashier who shakes her head after looking at us? Or pinch the woman with her three small children after she hurries them all past? And what about the woman cutting large swaths of material, the way she keeps staring, not even bothering to look away when I meet her eyes. I'd have to beat up this whole town for hurting Laura, embarrassing my mothers.

I hug Laura's neck, kiss her face.

"We'll ignore them all," I say. "Like Mother Claire said."

Laura nods.

My mothers are getting fabric for new nightgowns for all the girls and pajamas for the boys, cotton for shirts and dresses, and last of all, a simple white fabric with a white eyelet coverlet that will make my wedding dress a little less plain.

During all this shopping, Laura, Mariah, and I wander the store. We look at the DMC threads and talk about maybe getting a pattern for cross-stitching. We look at the fabric paints and the scrapbooking paper. Near the dried flowers I think, only for a moment, what's going on with Joshua?

Has he gone to the Prophet?

The material that they're picking out right now, is it for my marriage to Uncle Hyrum. Or to Joshua?

"You know what?" Laura says near the patterns. She isn't embarrassed anymore. "I don't think I could wear anything in here."

Mother Sarah has found a pattern for my dress. Long sleeved, to the floor, high on the neck, the eyelet material covering it all. (Joshua? Is it going well?)

"I know what you mean," I say. I hold Mariah now. She slaps at the models in the McCall's pattern book.

"Can you believe this?" Laura points to a purple satin dress. The back is bare, and the front plunges low. I'm surprised I can't see the model's belly button.

"Or this?" I say, tapping a picture of a girl in a short skirt. Mariah grabs my hand and I kiss her face. "How do girls wear stuff like this?"

Laura shrugs. Then she draws her hands into claws, and in a deep voice says, "It's Satan."

I laugh. Mariah laughs, too, like she understands what we're talking about.

In the van on the way to Applebee's, I wonder if this, the stores and people milling about and tattoos, is really all influenced by Satan and his Dark Angels. *Can it be,* I wonder, a new thought, a scary thought, *that everyone in the world is wrong, and just The Chosen Ones are right?* There are so few of us and billions of them.

ONCE, two years after Prophet Childs took over and closed us into our community, people started peering in.

"They are Satan," Prophet Childs told us.

Television crews came, men and women to interview him. He said he would talk to no one unless God instructed him to do so. God never did tell the Prophet to talk to them.

Lots of people stopped by to watch when the fence went up. Families in cars and old couples and the reporters. They all stared as the men and boys dug holes and mixed concrete and set the chain-link fence at the front of our property. Week after week they came, begging for interviews. They were met with the God Squad, guns on their hips, black suits, no matter the weather.

"When you see them, with their all-seeing eyes, with those cameras, you run," Prophet Childs told us during meetings. "They are Satan, here to try and steal you from us. To take babies from their mothers' breasts. To teach you the ways of the world. To lead you all to hell."

I cried when Prophet Childs warned us.

"Father, they want to take us from you." And Father would hold me, pet my face, pull Laura onto his lap, kiss our cheeks. "They can't take you away," he said. "I'm here."

I had seen the men and women, coming close to the fence, filming. So I ran.

"Laura!" I screamed for her. Grabbed at her, grabbed at Emily to bring her along, and ran away from the cameras. For a while we couldn't go outside without the eyes of the world, all those cameras, watching. I quit walking, quit going to my tree.

And I dreamed. Of Satan, with black horns on his head and eyes red as fire.

"Mother," I cried out more than once in the night.

"What, Kyra?"

"Satan's in my room. In the closet."

"He's not," she'd say, and turn on the light to show me.

Another night. "He's under my bed."

Another. "I saw him at the window."

"I'm here," Mother said every time. "I'm here. You're safe. No one's taking you away from me."

"WE HAVE TO HURRY," Mother Claire says when we sit down for lunch in Applebee's. "We have to get you home in time for your meeting with Brother Hyrum."

"Please," I say, my voice sounding sharp. "Don't remind me."

"Watch your tone," she says.

Laura lets out a sigh.

I am sure Mother Claire's words have ruined my appetite until the waitress sets a plate of chicken and shrimp in front of me. This food is so delicious I can hardly stand it.

"No wonder you wanted to come here," I say to Mother Victoria and she smiles so big I can see her back teeth.

The five of us, plus Mariah in a high chair, sit at a round table. It's the first time, I realize, that I've seen our mothers all sitting at the same time, not including church services.

"You're laughing and smiling," Laura says to them.

They look at us, then at each other, and they grin.

"I don't want to marry Uncle Hyrum," I say. I blurt this out right as a waitress passes with a pitcher of water.

Mother Sarah, her belly hidden by the table, says, "Not now, Kyra."

Mother Victoria holds her finger to her lips.

"We do what God says," Mother Claire says. And I know *she* does because she let my uncle discipline her baby.

"I don't want to," I say.

Laura is quiet, looking at her broccoli and noodles. She's chosen something Asian to eat.

"If I can't tell you three, who do I tell? Father can't change it." My voice grows quiet and I say what disgusts me. "I don't want to have my uncle's babies. I don't even want him touching me."

"Kyra!" Laura says, her voice shocked.

124

"We don't speak of that," Mother says. Her face turns pink. "That is sacred. Never meant for anyone but a husband and his wife."

Panic rises in my chest. I grip my fork. "I don't want to," I say. "I don't care if we don't talk about it. Father was young when you married him, Mother Claire. And still young when you married him, Mother."

Mother Claire looks away, over my head.

"And Uncle Hyrum is Father's oldest brother. He's . . . he's . . ."

"Horrible," Laura says. "It's not fair."

I hear laughter from another table. Do they know now? I don't care if they do.

"You'll learn," Mother Claire says.

"I won't," I say. Then I look all my mothers right in their eyes. "I won't do it."

The happy feeling at the table is gone.

"You'll do as you're told," Mother Victoria says. But her voice isn't strong like Mother Claire's would be if she'd said this.

I shake my head.

I will *not* do it, I think.

Ever.

THREE WEEKS AFTER my first kiss with Joshua, the Prophet spoke of marriage during a special meeting for pre-teens and teens.

"Woman," he said, "woman is made for man."

I couldn't help myself. I looked right at Joshua, my face flaming. He glanced at me, a small smile on his lips, then turned back to the Prophet.

"This is from God," Prophet Childs said. "This is prophecy. Girls, you are to be a subservient partner to your husband. You and your sister wives will raise a mighty generation of your own children unto the Lord."

I looked at Laura. She had tears in her eyes. She's so devoted. So good.

The room was hot. My tights felt like they were strangling my waist. I must have put them on crooked.

"There are men here just for you," Prophet Childs said.

I closed my eyes so I wouldn't look at Joshua. Opened them again.

"And here's the best thing." Prophet Childs smiled. He smiled and his whole face lit up. His eyes shone in the bright lights of the room.

"Brother Arnold. Brother Bennion. Brothers Hunter, Marshall, and Cox. All these good men, and several others, can give a life to you young girls who are nearing the age for marriage. A life that will exalt you here on earth"—Prophet Childs pointed at the wooden floor—

"and in the life to come." He pointed at the ceiling.

"Boys, they are your example to follow. Like Jesus."

The Prophet took in a breath. "Girls, you *will* obey. God has thus spoken."

BY THE TIME we get home I just have enough time to shower. "Come talk to me," I say to Laura.

She sits on the toilet while I undress behind the shower curtain and throw my clothes over.

"I don't know how I'm going to do it," I say.

"I wish I could go with you," she says. "Stay with you."

"Marry him, too?" I say through the hot water. It's almost funny to be able to tease her like this.

"Never," she says. "I hope that never happens to me."

I peer out behind the curtain. "Me, too." And I mean it. "Me, too."

Sometimes, two or three sisters will marry the same husband, one after the other. Brother Nelson, one of the God Squad, married all five of Brother Hennessy's daughters. When Brother Hennessy said something about it, he was told to leave the Compound and to never come back. He had to leave. Without any of his family. They all stayed behind.

"HOW OLD ARE YOU NOW, Kyra?" Uncle Hyrum asks. His thin hands work at a napkin he holds at the table.

"Thirteen," I say. Mother Claire braided my hair so tight for this meeting, this *date,* that I feel tears threatening to leak from my eyes. My knees are weak and I'm sitting. What would happen if I stood right now?

Uncle Hyrum nods. "That's good," he says.

Aunt Melissa places a plate in front of him. The food is piled high. The room fills with the smell of baked chicken. But Aunt Melissa sure doesn't look like she cares. Her mouth is thin, like someone took a red pen and made a line where her lips should be.

She goes back to the kitchen and brings out my plate. She sets it before me.

"Thank you," I say, but she doesn't answer.

There's a chicken leg and a chicken wing on the flowered plate. The pile of mashed potatoes is the size of a fifty-cent piece. The ear of corn is missing so many kernels I know it should go to the pigs and not me.

I try to catch Aunt Melissa's stare. I want to say to her, "I don't want to do this any more than you want me to," but I can't.

She goes to the kitchen and comes back again with a platter full of bread.

"I have the place where we'll stay," Uncle Hyrum says as

Aunt Melissa fills the table with food. Uncle Hyrum's house is huge and roomy. And he has a piano, too.

He reaches for my hand, but I move away. Still he grabs me, his grip tight. I make a fist. My stomach clenches.

"We'll be wed in just a few weeks."

I want to say, "Joshua's going to change this. He's going to make it right." I want to scream, "I'll never marry you." I want to stand up and run fast as I can away from here, from him. Instead, I stare at the bones in his hand. Black hair grows from the knuckles. Does Father have black hair like that?

I keep my mouth shut. Maybe my mouth is the same almost-line that Aunt Melissa's is. Maybe we are all-the-sudden twins.

"Soon, Kyra," Uncle Hyrum says, "you'll be a part of this eternal family. And we'll live together in glory forever."

Aunt Melissa puts out a pitcher of milk. Then she stands back, staring off over the top of my head. She's old and her face is wrinkled. I used to think she was nice. Before tonight, I mean.

"Let us pray," Uncle Hyrum says. It's just the three of us in the room.

Joshua, I think. *Joshua.*

———

AFTER DINNER, Uncle Hyrum says he'll walk me home.

"I can go alone," I say. "It's not that far."

"Kyra," he says. His voice is sharp.

His house is beautiful. The kitchen has five refrigerators. The granite countertops gleam. There are windows everywhere. The house is silent, though I know people must be here. Where is everyone?

We walk past a living room that has pale green carpet in it. A huge fireplace takes up one wall.

"This is how an Apostle lives," Uncle Hyrum says. "God does bless the righteous. And those who are saved and chosen for them."

I say nothing.

Out the door we go. It's late evening, and the sky is heavy with low clouds. Uncle Hyrum turns and points to a bay window on the second floor. "That's our wedding room, Kyra," he says and tries to take my hand again.

"Oh," I say. I quicken my step, avoiding him, and head toward home.

"Take it slow," Uncle Hyrum says. "We have plenty of time." He grabs my arm, links us together.

I fight the urge to run screaming all the way to my family. I can't see the world around me, I feel so sick. I trip once, and Uncle Hyrum keeps me from falling flat on my face. "A little klutzy, are you? Well, it's a good thing I'm here."

He clears his throat. "There's no need to be scared of me, Kyra. I'm a good husband. I'll keep real good care of you. You'll have the nicest things."

"Okay," I say. My heart feels like it's trying to escape.

"Good." In the light of the Temple, I see Uncle Hyrum smile. There *must* be something good about him. There *must*. Look how Aunt Melissa seems to love him.

"I take real excellent care of my wives," Uncle Hyrum says when we get to my front porch. He pulls me close to him. His arms are like steel rods. "I'm gentle with the new ones."

"What are you doing?" I say. Fear rises right up my throat.

"No use in fighting me, Kyra," Uncle Hyrum says, breathing potato breath on me. "No matter what, I'll get my way."

I struggle. His arms tighten. He's a head taller than me. And much too close. This is not a thing what it feels like when Joshua holds me near.

"It's God's law that I have you."

"No," I say. "Mother! Not now. Not yet."

"Kiss me good night."

"No!" I push hard against Uncle Hyrum.

Then Father is there.

"You're not married to her yet, Hyrum," he says and reaches his hand to me.

My uncle releases his hold, straightens his shirt. "Fighting won't do anything but make it worse. Fighting won't do anything but make it harder. Tell her that, Richard."

WAS FATHER THAT WAY to my mother the first night he slept with her? Did he force his love on her? Did she fight him?

Oh, how am I ever going to do this?

WHEN EVERYONE IS ASLEEP, I drop to my knees and claw under the bed. My fingertips feel greasy and no matter how many times I wash them I can't lose the feeling. It's like the chicken is stuck there and will never go away.

There's a backpack under my bed, an old orange one. I'm going to pack it up with stuff and I'm leaving. If Joshua's talk with the Prophet didn't work out, I'm leaving.

Bill did it.

I can, too.

"Kyra?" Laura leans up in bed.

"What?" I don't mean to be so loud, but she's scared me. There it is! I've found the backpack.

Laura peers over at me. "How was it?"

For a moment I think of Uncle Hyrum walking me to our front door. Of Father . . . Father rescuing me.

"Awful," I say. My voice is a whisper. "Worse than anything you can think." I'm still on my knees. I wipe my fingers on the sheet.

"Why?"

I can see my sister, my best friend, leaning toward me. Her hair is loose and has fallen over her shoulders. I love her so much I'd do just about anything to save her. Gazing at my sister, with just the hall night-light coming into our room, words spin through my head.

Why are we here? How did we get here? How do we get out of here?

What have our father and mother done to us?

It's this last sentence that sticks right in my lungs. After a minute, I climb up next to Laura.

"Roll over," I say, "and I'll scrooch up next to your back."

She does. I slip my arms around her. She's warm and thin and bony. She's just a baby. When will *she* have to get married?

"What happened?" she asks.

I can't answer right away. Then I pull in a deep breath. "When he tried to kiss me good night, I put my hands up."

"He tried to kiss you?"

"I wouldn't let him."

Now Laura says, "I wouldn't let him kiss me, either, if you want to know."

We say nothing. Outside a steady wind blows across the desert. I can smell the shampoo in Laura's hair. I can smell my own sweat.

"I've been thinking," Laura says. She lowers her voice. "I don't want to marry an old man either. Especially if he was my uncle." She pauses. "If we could, I'd choose for myself."

I squeeze my eyes shut, then nod and say, "Let's not talk about it anymore."

Sisters, I know, are supposed to be together till the end. I press my lips to the back of Laura's head in a kiss good night. I try to sleep.

I REMEMBER HOLDING LAURA. Mother's telling me the story keeps the memory alive, like it is my own. We were both so small. Mother sat near us, helping me support this new baby's head. Someone snapped a picture of us, the three of us together.

"Isn't she beautiful?" my mother said. Her voice was sweet against the side of my face.

"No," I said.

And Laura wasn't. Her face was red and squishy. Her hands curled up into fists. When she opened her eyes, there was no color at all.

Mother Sarah laughed. "Oh, Kyra," she said.

I DON'T WANT to leave my family.

This is the first thing I think when I open my eyes and stare at the ceiling the next morning.

I don't want to leave my family.

This is the first thing I think at breakfast.

Carolina is grumpy. But when she sees me she comes running straight into my arms. I kiss her face over and over.

Margaret hums something from church. She dances a bit as she sets the table. Then she hugs me tight, too.

Laura stares, like she wants to pat away my sadness the way she does with all Father's babies.

I don't want to leave my family.

Maybe I will never think anything else.

I have no choice. In less than a month, I leave this home to join with Uncle Hyrum's family. In less than a month, I'll never sleep beside my sister again.

But if I run . . .

Mother and Father are in their room. I can hear them talking. What is he telling her?

The house smells of oatmeal with brown sugar sprinkled on it. The room is cool from night. The early morning sun has colored the sky in the east a pale blue.

I want to scream. I want to scream and run to Prophet

Childs. I want to tell him, "Leave me with my family. Leave me with my mother and my sisters. Leave me home."

But what would he say?

God's will be done.

That's it.

I know it.

HOW CAN I go to Uncle Hyrum?

Kiss his greasy lips?

Taste the chicken?

Let his hands touch my body?

There is so little time left for me.

How can I do this?

I've got to get away.

AFTER BREAKFAST, I pull out the sewing machine. We clear the table and set up there. "Let's cut out the pattern in the living room," Mother says. She folds the fabric in half, lays it on the floor.

I think of the beautiful green carpet in Uncle Hyrum's house. Here, the carpet is old and so worn at the front door and near the bedroom doors that you can almost see to the pad below.

"Do we have to do this today?" I ask.

"Just the cutting," Mother says. Then she puts her arms around me. And without a word, all three of my sisters fall into the hug, too.

"It's going to be okay," Mother says. Her voice is like a prayer. The baby in her belly gives me a kick.

"I don't want Kyra to leave," Margaret says.

"Me either," says Carolina and she bursts into loud tears.

"Me either," says Laura.

There's a knock at the door. Mother wipes at her face with the back of her hand and goes to answer it.

It's Sheriff Felix.

"What?" I say. My first thought is Patrick. But he can't be out there now. He won't be back for days.

My second thought is Josh. I don't move.

"Kyra Leigh. The Prophet wants to see you."

"Now?" I say.

He nods.

"Whatever for?" Mother says. "And why so early in the morning?"

Sheriff Felix ignores her.

"Let me change," I say.

"No," he says. "Come now. As you are."

I hurry to the door. Mother does, too.

"I'll take her, Sister," the sheriff says.

"I'm coming, too," Mother says. "I need to know what's happening with my daughter." Mother's face has grown pale.

"The Prophet has asked for Sister Kyra. Alone."

"Get your father," Mother says to Laura, who doesn't even ask why, just runs out the back door.

Mother hugs me again, as I walk away from home and into the morning. It's cool outside. The sky is a thin blue. We only have two blocks, if that, to go. But my knees shake so, I don't think I can make it.

"Why does he want me?" I ask Sheriff Felix.

Was it because I wouldn't kiss Uncle Hyrum? Did he *tattle* on me? Can the Prophet decide who I kiss before I marry?

The thought turns me cold, inside and out. By the time we get to the Temple, I'm shaking all over.

I'VE NEVER BEEN in the upper rooms of the Temple before, except once on a dare. And the God Squad chased me out. Now, I wait in the front room.

Through the huge plate-glass windows I can see everything. Our whole Compound. The Prophet's and Apostles' homes scattered farther out. The home where I will live when I marry Uncle Hyrum. The lush green of their lawns. And past that to the trailers where all of The Chosen Ones live. I can imagine seeing my home if I close my eyes.

A door swings open.

"Sister Kyra."

It's Uncle Hyrum.

It feels like my lungs leap into my throat. I can't even breathe. Can barely nod at him. My feet have stopped working. My heart, though, is beating double time. Maybe like a hummingbird's.

For a brief second I remember reading the hummingbird book while sitting on the floor of the Ironton County Mobile Library on Wheels. I can feel my legs tucked under me as I turn the pages and see the ruby-throated hummingbird for the first time.

"Prophet Childs will see you."

Uncle Hyrum's tone is that of ice.

Somehow I follow him. Down a hall we go. Portraits hang on the walls. Portraits of Jesus and Prophet Childs's father and the Prophet before him and the one before him. There's a painting of Prophet Childs himself, standing on the right hand of Jesus. They're smiling at each other.

The carpet is thick under my feet. The hall is air-conditioned so low that I rub my arms to smooth down the goose bumps. Mother would feel comfortable in a place like this. She wouldn't be so hot.

"In here," Uncle Hyrum says.

The room is huge. A whole wall of windows look out on the Temple. There are three computers. Two walls of books. A huge television. Dark green carpet. A desk so large I could sleep on it with Laura *and* Carolina.

Prophet Childs stands next to the window, gazing at the Compound. His hands are clasped behind himself. He rocks on his feet in his shiny shoes.

Standing near the back wall are Brother Laramie and Brother Nelson, two members of the God Squad. And in a chair is Joshua. My Joshua.

"WHO ELSE DO YOU LIKE?" I asked Joshua one late night. The moon was a sliver, hanging low in the sky like it was caught in a fall.

"What?" Joshua's voice was hushed.

We'd finished *Harry Potter* and I wanted to play with magic. I was sure I would be good at it.

"What other girl do you like?"

I turned to him. I could just see the outline of his face. If we moved just a few inches to the left we'd be in the false light of the Temple spire.

"That's out of the blue," Joshua said. He held the book on his lap.

"I know," I said.

"Why are you asking?" Joshua shifted until his head rested on my shoulder. I could see his tennis shoe. A bit of one sock.

"You have to have three wives to get into heaven," I said. "You know that. Do you have two other choices?"

Am I worth going to hell for? I thought, but I didn't say the words. Because what if I would go to hell for Joshua but he wouldn't for me?

He was quiet.

"You have to be with three women. Kiss them. Love them." I made my voice all singsongy though my words made me feel jealous and itchy inside. "Have babies with them."

The darkness made me powerful. Or was it *Harry Potter?* Had magic seeped from the book into me, making me stronger? Less afraid? Bold enough to say these words to Joshua?

"I know what they say," Joshua said.

I lowered my voice. "Do you believe it?"

He shrugged. I felt his shoulders lift and settle again. The movement caused the smell of soap to float toward me.

"Do you ever think about it?"

He shrugged a second time. Again that smell.

"I don't think of other girls," Joshua said. "I don't think of having three wives. I think of you."

I clamped my mouth shut in case the magic made me tell that I was sure I loved him.

"Kyra," he said after a long moment. "I choose you. Only."

I ALMOST CRY OUT when I see Joshua. His face is a mess. They've beat him good.

He doesn't look at me.

"Kyra Leigh Carlson," Prophet Childs says, still staring out those big windows. He doesn't look at me. He just watches out the windows. Below, people are coming to life, men heading toward fields, some women hanging washed clothes on lines to dry. "Do you understand what adultery is?"

"Umm," I say.

I can't look away from Joshua. He's so bruised I want to go to him. Smooth his face with my hands. Touch his split lips with my mouth. Comfort him with hugs. I feel too shocked to answer.

"Adultery is lusting after someone you are not meant to be with," Prophet Childs says.

Now he turns. I look at the Prophet. There is no smile on his face. No warmth there. What I see scares me.

"God has chosen who you are to marry," Prophet Childs

142

says. "In the belly of the Temple, He let me know the man you will spend eternity with. And you have been with this boy."

"We didn't do anything," Joshua says.

"You asked for her hand," Prophet Childs said. "You said you loved her. You met her after dark."

Prophet Childs walks toward me. Without meaning to, I back up.

"I would never have an adulteress as a wife," he says.

I swallow.

"What you have done is an abomination. Women were stoned for less in the Bible," he says.

All at once I think I'm going to die. They are going to kill me the way they did Ellen. The way they killed Sister Janie's tiny baby.

"I didn't do anything," I say.

Uncle Hyrum slaps me with the back of his hand. Tears sting my eyes and my nose starts to run. I actually see stars.

"Ow," I say.

"No," Joshua says, leaping to his feet.

Brother Laramie hits Joshua so hard in the face blood splatters against the wall. He falls to the floor and I run to him, but Uncle Hyrum catches me in his arms. How can he be so strong? How can he be so old and so strong? He's pinned my arms to my sides. But I struggle anyway, kicking at his shins, twisting this way and that.

The Prophet is in my face. I can smell his breath. It's sweet as sugar. "If he will have you, you will be free." The words come out slow, one-at-a-time slow.

At first I think Joshua, if Joshua will have me, then I'll be free. Uncle Hyrum sets me loose and looks at me with such an angry glare that I realize the "he" is my uncle. For a moment I have hope. Uncle Hyrum is so angry. So angry.

Maybe, just maybe, I won't have to marry him.

Maybe, just maybe, God has heard my prayers and I'm safe.

Maybe, just maybe, I can be with Joshua.

"Apostle Carlson, will you still take the girl?"

I look to my uncle, whose arms are like bands, shaking my head. My nose is still running. I wipe my lip and when I pull my hand away, I see blood.

"I can keep her in line," he says after a few moments. "I've trained the others. I can train her."

I don't know why, but my knees give out. I fall to the floor. From where I'm lying, I can see Joshua. He reaches for me. He's bleeding and his eye is swollen shut. I crawl fast as I can to him, reaching his hand, grabbing it for a moment. A shiny shoe smashes into our hands and I scream.

"This isn't truth," Joshua says, pushing himself up. "None of this is. We didn't do anything."

"Blasphemer," Uncle Hyrum says. His voice is a hiss, the way a snake might sound if it could talk.

144

For a second I think of Satan, and that snake in the Garden of Eden. Did he sound like Uncle Hyrum does?

"You don't beat people to keep them in line," Joshua says. I'm not sure how he gets to his feet, he's that hurt, and seeing him like this, because of me, makes me weep. I sob. He's next to me in a moment, touching my hair, pulling me to my feet.

"Take him away," Prophet Childs says.

"No!" I say. I'm loud. I put my arms around Joshua's waist and hold tight to him.

"Wait, wait," Joshua says. "Just listen."

But they don't. Brother Nelson and Brother Laramie reach for Joshua. It's a short tug-of-war as they pull him away from me. They wrench his arm up behind him.

"Stop it!" I'm screaming. "Let him go!"

Joshua swears and shouts how this is not God's true church. "God would never demand this," he says, and his voice is all alone in the room.

There's not another sound until Prophet Childs says, "Get thee behind me, Satan."

And he turns his back on Joshua and looks out the window toward the Temple again.

I try to follow as they drag Joshua away. I throw myself after him.

"Run," Joshua says to me. "Get free, Kyra. Find me. Find me when you can. I'll be waiting."

"I'm going with him," I say to Prophet Childs. I try to run past Uncle Hyrum, but he grabs me again.

"Let me go." My voice is one I don't recognize.

The door closes.

For a minute I think I might scream every bit of life out of me. But I bite my tongue.

"The ceremony will still be," Prophet Childs says.

"I won't do it," I say.

The Prophet looks back out his big window. I wonder how the God Squad will get Joshua out of this building without being seen. Or maybe they don't care who sees what they've done. Of course they don't. Standing here, I remember more than one person paraded down the street for others to see. To teach us all a lesson. Sometimes those people showed up in church meetings. Sometimes we never saw them again. Not a lot of people. Mostly The Chosen Ones do what they are told. But I'm not so sure I can.

"Only you can save him," Prophet Childs says after a few quiet moments.

My whole body goes cold. "What do you mean?" My voice is a whisper.

Uncle Hyrum rocks back on his heels, but the scowl never leaves his face. He squeezes my wrists in his hands. Pinches at my skin.

"Only you can save Joshua Johnson," Prophet Childs says. He doesn't look at me. Just keeps staring out at the Temple.

I say nothing.

"You marry who God has chosen for you to marry."

"You do as God tells you to do."

"You are obedient."

Now Prophet Childs turns and faces me.

"Or else."

The Prophet looks at Uncle Hyrum. "Discipline?" he says.

Uncle Hyrum gives just one nod of his head. "Girl, you have your first lesson to learn right now," Uncle Hyrum says and he balls his hands into fists.

WHEN THE BEATING STARTS, I think of Mozart. Concentrate on Mozart. Wish for Mozart to come back from the dead and sweep me away.

MY FACE IS BRUISED, one eye closing shut, both lips busted, split wide-open. I feel that with my tongue.

"The lesson of the kingdom," Uncle Hyrum says. He wipes his hands on a towel that one of the God Squad brought him. "Be glad it isn't worse, Miss Kyra."

I'm too busy crying to answer.

The Prophet doesn't even look my way, just dismisses us both with a wave like he's grown bored.

MOTHER FAINTS when she sees me. Laura screams and runs for help. I lie down on the sofa and Margaret hurries to the bathroom. I hear her running water. She comes back with a wet cloth.

"Here," she says. I can almost not hear her voice.

Carolina looks at me with wide eyes, then starts crying. Then my other mothers are there. Mother Victoria rushes to my mother, who looks like a broken doll, that braid twisting away from her head like a rope. Mother Claire pulls me onto her lap. Tears fall from her eyes.

"Kyra," she says.

Please, I think. *No more preaching. No more.* I wonder if I will have to use Mozart to drown her out. I wonder if he will be with me again.

"I tried to run," she says, her voice a whisper.

I grow paper-thin. This woman, the meanest of my father's wives, *she* tried to get away?

Her voice is low in my ear.

I look at her through one eye. I hear Mother Victoria murmuring to my mother, hear her go into the kitchen and start herbs to boiling on the stove.

"There's no getting away." Mother Claire strokes my hair, touches her lips to my bruises, lets her finger trace the cuts. "I tried three times. They meant to break me. But the man who was supposed to be my husband, he wouldn't have me. Called me wild. Said I was a whore. So I got your father instead. A blessing if ever there was any."

Her voice is like cotton. Her fingers almost not there. I must be lost.

Mother Claire puts her arms around me. "I'm here," she says.

She hums, and I lean against her shoulder, letting her rock me.

FATHER COMES RUNNING into our home, slinging the door open.

"What in the hell?" he says when he sees me. "Who did this, Kyra?" He kneels before me, still cradled in Mother Claire's arms.

"Hyrum," Mother Claire says.

He leaves. And is gone for hours. The sun has set.

Finn brings a rumor that Sheriff Felix will be running several boys off the Compound. *Please,* I think, though my prayers haven't helped me at all, *please let Joshua still be alive.*

Mother goes to bed with Carolina and Margaret. My

other mothers go home to their families. I stay up, sitting in the dark, waiting for Father. There's a knock on the door, then Emily walks in, grinning until she sees my face.

"Oh Kyra, oh Kyra," she says. "Mother said to visit. She did. She said to visit. She says to tell you."

"Tell me what, Emily?" I say.

Laura comes into the living room with us. She turns on the light over the stove, opens the oven door so that light shines too. Outside a soft wind blows. Someone's dog barks like crazy, then stops with a yelp.

Emily, simple Emily, hovers near me. She kisses my hairline.

"Kyra," she says, her speech slurred. She leans into my face. "Jesus is listening to you."

"He is?" Tears spring to my eyes. I stare at my sister, seeing how she looks a little like Laura.

"He told me to tell you," Emily says. "He knows you here." She touches my chest where my heart is. "And here." She touches my forehead. Then she whispers, "He loves you. No hell for you."

She kisses at my face until Father comes home.

"Laura," Father says, "walk Miss Emily home, then hurry up to bed yourself."

They both hug him good night.

"Let's sit outside," he says to me.

We go out on the back porch. I can feel the worn wood under my feet. I can hear the chickens settling in for the evening.

"Sit down," Father says. He puts his arm around my shoulder, pulls me close. I can smell leftover aftershave on him. I close my eyes and breathe deep the smell of my father. I'm leaning against his shoulder, just resting, just loving him, just wishing he could save me when he says, "Do you remember what happened to Brother Alex Delango?"

The smell of sage breezes past. "Yes," I say.

"Do you remember how he lost everything because he dared to contradict Prophet Childs?"

We sit for a moment, the quiet and cool night air between us.

"They took his children and wives and gave them to two other of the brethren. They made him leave, along with Brother Olsen and Brother Adamson. The three of them were run off, all of them losing their families because they crossed the Prophet. Do you remember?"

I nod. "Yes sir."

"Do you remember how those fathers were to those new wives and children?"

Again, I nod.

The night sky is full of stars. They look close enough to reach. If I didn't hurt so much, I bet I could touch one.

Father and I don't say anything else. We sit there, quiet. But I know what he's telling me.

    I have to do what they say.

    Or he loses everything.

III

Mother Sarah isn't feeling good again. She's not throwing up, but her face stays slick with sweat. Her skin has grown pale except for two spots of pink in her cheeks. Her lips are dry. She doesn't even get out of bed.

But I can only think of myself. I hurt all over. Bruises have appeared on both arms, my legs, and across my back. When did that happen? I can't remember Uncle Hyrum hitting me anywhere but in the face and head. I have a headache that gets worse when the sun shines in my eyes.

I draw the curtains and whisper at my sisters, "Let's keep it down today, okay?"

Laura, Margaret, and Carolina *are* quiet. We work together making breakfast and when I go to step outside and work in the garden, Margaret says, "I'll do your part today." I would kiss her, but my lips seep blood.

There's a knock at the door and Mother Claire comes in. She cringes when she sees my face, then glances away.

"I'm here to pin that dress to you," she says.

I gather the pieces of material Mother cut out. When did she do this? While she was waiting for me to come back from seeing the Prophet? While she was waiting for Father?

I think of her on her knees on the floor, cutting the material for my wedding dress with her scissors given to her by her mother.

"Let's go, Miss Kyra," Mother Claire says.

I move to her and she picks up this and that, pinning at my shoulders, under my arms, down the back.

"Stand on the chair," she says.

I do and she pins up the hem.

My voice comes out low. "I don't love him," I say.

Mother Claire is silent.

"Not as an uncle. Not as a husband."

"You'll learn," Mother Claire says.

I look down at her. From here I can see that some of her hair is turning gray. How can that be?

"You'll learn to love him." She says this around straight pins she holds between her lips. "If you put your heart in God's hands."

"I want my heart where it is," I say, tapping my chest.

"You'll learn," she says.

"We do what we have to do," she says.

"I did it," she says.

I look into Mother Claire's face. She's worried for me, I can see it. With the back of her hand, she smooths my face where there is no hurt. I close my eyes at her touch.

THAT NIGHT MOTHER GOES into labor. I know without anyone saying anything it's because of the way I look. Because of what happened to me. I can't even go in the bedroom with her. Every time Mother sees me, she cries. Mother Claire, petting me, sends me out. She and Mother Victoria take turns sitting with my mother while Mother calls out.

"Something's wrong!"

I hear Mother say this, hear the words early Sunday morning. Mother Victoria is with her. She mumbles something.

"There's something wrong with the baby."

I run to Mother's bedroom door. Look in at her. Her hair is damp, stuck to her face. The sight of her scares me. Her words scare me.

"What is it?" Laura says. She's pushed past me.

"Go out," Mother Victoria says. She's working between Mother's legs. The blankets, the covers, are twisted. Mother's knees are like a girl's. "Get Father."

Laura turns, runs.

Mother, her whole face screwed up, looks at me. Just once. She screams.

"Out," Mother Victoria says.

I run for my tree.

I SAW HER.

Perfect. Hands and fingers. Feet and toes. Red. Skinny. Too skinny. Struggling to breathe.

She gasped for air, that baby, fighting for a moment to live.

"Please, Victoria. Please, Claire," Mother said. "I've lost too many. Please."

"She's not going to make it, Sarah," Mother Claire said.

"Her name is Abigail," Mother said.

I wept near the dresser. Laura and Margaret crowded near me. Carolina was with Emily.

156

Then Father came in, walked past like we weren't there.

"Abigail," Mother said.

"Not now, Richard," Mother Claire said. She worked over that baby. Worked the best she could.

But Father ignored her and fell to his knees next to the bed, where the sheets were twisted and wet, where the towels were spattered with blood. The room smelled like birthing babies, and my mother looked too worn to breathe herself.

I stared at Abigail. A baby six months in the womb would survive outside of this place. I knew it to be true. I'd seen it in the newspapers Patrick brought. Hospitals that saved premature babies.

When Abigail pulled in her last breath, never making a sound, but twisting and fighting to breathe, when Mother, heartbroken, cried out, I left the room.

Now, I was a murderer, too.

IN MY DREAM, snow pelts against the window. Tapping and tapping. The wind whispers my name, Kyra.

I awake with my heart sitting on the back of my tongue.

"Kyra." The tapping sounds again. "Wake up."

It's Joshua at my window.

What?

"What are you doing out here?" I whisper. I crawl to my knees, press my face to the screen.

"I'm leaving, Kyra," he says. "I've got to go. They came by our house tonight."

Joshua's so upset that his voice shakes. In the near dark I can see the bruises.

A fat selfish part of me rears up. What will I do with him gone? "You can't go," I say.

"They're making me."

"Who?" I'm so close to the screen I smell dust. I don't even care if Laura wakes up.

"The Prophet. The Apostles. The God Squad. They're sending a bunch of us away. Me because I asked to Choose you."

It feels like a stool has been pushed from under my feet. I'm sliding sideways in all this.

He presses his forehead into the screen. We are separated only by the mesh. I can feel his skin. Smell him through the dust. "The girls here are for all the older men. They told me that yesterday." He takes a breath.

"Where will you go?"

For a moment he's quiet. "We've heard there's a safe house. We'll try for that."

I say, "Let me come with you."

"I just wanted to tell you good-bye," Joshua says. His voice cracks.

158

Just like that, I'm crying. "Let me come with you," I say again.

"I'll come back for you," Joshua says. "If you want me to, Kyra."

There's a sound behind him, and for a moment I think someone from the God Squad is there. I feel sick to my stomach.

But there are two other boys with him. "We've got to go," one of them says. I think it's Randall Allred. "I told you we shouldn't stop here. We got to go. Now. They're only giving us so much time, then they're following."

"Let me come with you. I can get dressed. Wait for me."

"No!" says another voice I don't recognize. "She'll slow us down. We only have so long. We gotta move now, Johnson. Now!" The voice is urgent. Scared.

"I've got to go," Joshua says. He presses his hand to the screen and I put my hand on his. I can feel his warmth. And then he's gone.

"Come back for me," I whisper, watching him in the darkness. But I've no idea at all if he's heard me.

A SPECIAL MEETING'S called.

"Hurry," Mother says from her bed. "You have to go without me."

159

Where is the baby?

"Are you still hurting?" Laura asks as we hurry to the Fellowship Hall. Her eyes are red from crying over Abigail. Little Abigail. So small.

I squint in the light, feel weak from pain, from not sleeping much, from crying.

There are murmurs all around. We divide ourselves, women on one side of the room, men on the other. The air conditioner blows in, cooling me.

"Children come forward," Brother Mathias says. "Come to the front. Sit close to our beloved Prophet."

They have moved a chair down for him, down from the stage so he can sit near us.

All the Apostles motion at us now, moving us forward with their fingers. Uncle Hyrum looks in my direction. He helps the children forward.

"Sit close," they say. "Sit close."

I've already settled near Mother Claire and I don't want to go closer to where the Prophet will be.

"You too, Kyra," Mother Victoria says. She smiles with her lips.

I'm reluctant, but I go forward, taking Mariah from Mother Claire so I can hold her on my lap.

Why am I here? How can I be here? My littlest sister is dead, my face is broken, the person I love is gone. How can

160

I sit here and pretend that I want to be in this room? I want to run.

Women near me look away. My face tells them I've been disobedient. I've been disciplined. It's plain to everyone.

We all settle down, all of us children, on the blue carpeted floor. Some of the kids play, some sit with little smiles on their faces.

Then Uncle Hyrum is on his feet. He starts singing, his voice rich and deep. Beautiful. I hate him. *"God sent the Prophet,"* he sings. *"God sent us the Prophet of all. Of all. To lead. To guide. To take us to heaven."*

People rise and clap as Prophet Childs comes in the room. He nods to us, lifts his hands to us, motions for us to sit. He takes his place in the maroon-colored chair, the microphone in his hands.

"I have been in prayer all morning," Prophet Childs says.

"Praise Jesus," a man calls from the back of the room.

"A Prophet prays for his people," Prophet Childs whispers these words.

"The word of God," another man cries out.

We're all quiet.

Mariah sits on my lap without moving. It feels like a rattlesnake winds around in my stomach. I concentrate on the blond of her hair. All the colors I see there. Near white. Three shades of yellow. A golden strand.

"He prays for his people. He wishes them no harm," Prophet Childs says.

Is he talking to me? He wishes *me* no harm?

His mouth is so close to the microphone I can hear his breath.

"But some children do wrong," he says.

I'm still not looking at anything but Mariah's hair. All that hair that's so fine to the touch. All that hair that's so curly she'll have a hard time keeping it in braids when she's older. Can she feel my heart beating in her back?

"Some of you have done wrong," he says.

My eyes can't see. I can only hear his words.

"This place we have here is to keep you safe from Satan. And he is outside our walls. Everywhere. On the street. In the stores. On the televisions and computers. Those people who do not believe what we believe, they carry Satan's lies and fabrications in their heads. They will kill you, if you even dare to look in their direction."

Prophet Childs pauses.

"Keep away from the outside," he says, "or it will burn you on the inside and on the outside."

He's on his feet now, I know without looking at him. He's moving closer.

"Keep away from Satan. He will destroy you."

He stands and walks amongst all of us on the floor. The room so wide you could throw a football across it. I know because Joshua did that very thing with a friend of his when they were supposed to be cleaning the room and making it ready for the Sabbath.

"Satan is in what we read, if we read anything but scriptures."

Does he know, I wonder, my sin of reading? I put my face close to Mariah.

"He is in our thoughts, if we think of any place outside of this sanctuary."

Does he know I want to leave now? That I'm planning to leave?

"He is looking for you."

Prophet Childs stands right before me now. He has made his way to me. I see his shoes, so shiny. Was it his foot that stepped on Joshua and me? Mariah reaches out for her reflection, and he moves back.

"Look up," he says.

Can he be telling me that? I look at Mariah and me in the toe of the shoe and see how dark we are. Grabbed by Satan already. Though Mariah couldn't be. Not yet. Isn't she too young?

"Kyra," Laura says, her whisper so slight I bet no one can hear it but me.

"Look up," the Prophet says again.

The whole room is dead quiet.

I look up. Way up. He's so tall when I'm here on the floor.

"Three boys ran last night." He says this to everyone, though he stares at me. I look at his ear.

"And we won't go looking for them."

Joshua. My heart pounds.

"They'll die in the desert."

I hear a woman draw in a gasp of air. Joshua's mother? One of the other boys'?

"Die of thirst and heat and soon the buzzards will pick their bones clean. They will die a sinner's death at the hands of God."

A light behind the Prophet shines around his head like a halo.

And right there in front of him, right where he stands so close he can maybe read my mind, I think, *Joshua will* not *die. He'll make it out of here for good. And he'll come back for me.*

That's when I look Prophet Childs in the eye.

He stops speaking. Stares at me. And I stare right back. Because I know in the center of my heart, in the place I've kept all our secret meetings and all my secret warm thoughts about Joshua, I know there that he *will* get away.

For what seems an eternity, Prophet Child stands above me, staring down.

Then he says, "You *will* be punished for breaking God's commandments."

I feel the touch of someone's hand to mine as the Prophet walks back to the front of the room and then dismisses us.

"WHY?" Mother Victoria says.

We are all at her trailer so that my mother can sleep.

"Why did he single Kyra out? Why did he stand over her like that? He said three boys ran last night. Why did he stare at *her*?"

"I don't know," I say. My lie burns at the back of my throat.

"What have you done?" she asks.

"Nothing. Nothing more than what you know."

But they know nothing. At least, I think they know nothing. I have said nothing of Joshua. This shame would be too much for my family. Maybe Mother Claire would also go into labor. Maybe she would lose her baby, too.

Abigail.

"Kyra," Father says. He leans close. "You know consequences can be severe. You know what they do to those who are disobedient."

I nod.

"Tell me," he says.

People run, I want to say. They go. They get away. But I say, "Amber Holdman was beaten when she ran and they brought her back." I can see Amber's face, so swollen her eyes wouldn't open, all that dark hair, those dark eyes just slits. She was supposed to marry Brother Felix. And she did, eventually. "And they've sent a lot of the boys away." I wonder if Father's thinking of his oldest boy, Adam. He's seventeen. But Father's tried hard to keep all his sons quiet and obedient.

"They drop some of the boys off in the desert," Mother Claire says. She stands, leaning against the dining room wall, her arms folded over her belly. "They leave them out there to die."

Mother Victoria says nothing. Just keeps her face down.

"If necessary they kill the unrighteous," Father said. "Blood sacrifice." He's taken my hands in both of his. "You must be obedient to God." His lips are thin with worry. I've never seen him like this. "My Kyra, we couldn't stand to lose you. We've lost too much already." His voice cracks in two and my father begins to cry. Out loud, cry. He folds in on himself, and his whole body shakes with despair. I hug him, as do his first two wives.

Father sobs out loud. Mother Victoria dips forward, encircling Father with her arms. "Shh," she says. "Shh."

Father says, "I always want you to be a part of our family, Kyra."

Mother Claire's eyes are squeezed shut, like she has a headache. Like maybe *I* am her headache.

There's a knock at the door.

Father tries to control his crying. As he wipes at his face, Mother Claire goes to the front door.

"Don't cry, Father," I say. My own tears threaten. I'm exhausted with the worry and death and fear of it all.

"Brother Carlson," a man's voice says. It's Prophet Childs.

Father stands, wiping at his face once more. I get to my feet.

Prophet Childs moves into the trailer, taking up all the good air.

I actually wince, then move behind Father. A scream edges up my throat, but I clamp it quiet behind my teeth.

"Sit," Father says, and he gestures to his own chair.

Prophet Childs just stands there. Father does, too.

Will he say something now? Will my father stand up for me?

"A man who cannot control his family does not deserve them," Prophet Childs says.

The Prophet looks at Father a good long while, then at me.

"If you can't keep your wild girls in line, Brother Carlson," Prophet Childs says, "we will give them to a man who can. You will lose this whole family if God finds you a failure. Do you understand?"

Father's face grows rigid, but he says nothing.

"We need to marry this child of yours off fast," Prophet

Childs says. "This wedding will come sooner than the others. Your brother is the man to care for this one and teach her obedience."

Father still says nothing.

"Punish the girl accordingly, Brother Carlson," Prophet Childs says. "Otherwise you will lose all there is. Your children. Your wives. And your place in heaven."

No one says a word. The air in the room is too heavy to shoulder. I stagger beneath it, falling onto the sofa.

"Punish her."

"I believe," Father says, and I can't see his face when he speaks, "that she's learned her lesson already."

Prophet Childs is quiet. "You have just this one chance," he says after a bit, "to make things right with God Almighty."

Mother Claire slips next to Father. She takes his hand, hardly making a move to do it. Mother Victoria stands next to Mother Claire. They are a line of bodies in front of me.

"Make her speak to you," Prophet Childs says, "then you might change your mind about the sin she has brought upon you all."

He leaves without shutting the door behind him.

There is no sound in the house except for the ticking of a clock. Emily wanders in from outside.

"I saw the Prophet," she says to Mother Victoria, hugging her mother with both arms.

She sees me on the sofa. "Oh, Kyra," she says. "Jesus wants you to know he'll take care of you."

Her words give me courage.

"Sit beside me, Emily," I say. She does. I take a breath. "I have to tell you something, Father."

I tell them about Joshua and me with Prophet Childs. I tell them how he was beaten. How he came by that night to tell me good-bye. I tell them I love him.

I leave out the parts where we kissed.

Leave out how we held hands.

Leave out how I would go to him right now, right now, if he came back for me.

If looks could melt, I'd be a goner. And not because they are angry at me. They are so shocked that all three stand looking down at me with their mouths open. Emily gives me a pat pat pat.

Mother Claire finds her way to her rocker and sits down. Mother Victoria just stares at me. Then she says, "Oh no, Kyra. Oh no."

Father shakes his head. Just keeps shaking his head. His eyes close and when he opens them again, he's still shaking his head. And Mother Victoria is a broken record, saying the same thing over and over. "Oh no. Oh no no nonononono."

"I didn't mean it," I say, holding my hands out to them like they might give me forgiveness if I wait long enough.

"Don't you understand?" Father says. "All the times

we've met together as a family? The way we've taught you to be wise. How could you *do* this?"

Mother Claire rocks. The chair lets out a slight squeaking sound. She looks away. "They're watching us now," she says. Then she glances at me, and in that look I know she understands what it is like to be in the eye of the Prophet.

Pat pat pat goes Emily's hand.

"Watching you and me and your mothers and your brothers and sisters," Father says. His voice is low.

"You've turned their attention to us," Mother Claire says. Still staring away.

I look out the window to our trailer, to where Mother lies sleeping. She has no idea. My whole face hurts. My back hurts. Everything hurts. Nothing I can say will fix what I have done. Nothing.

"They'll watch you forever, Kyra." Father's voice is worn out. Old. I think he might cry again, but he doesn't. But I know the way he feels, the fear he feels, is because of me. All because of me. "They'll watch you till they know you're broken."

"This," Father says, and he motions to me, "this is just the beginning." His voice cracks. "Kyra."

I put my arms around my father, even though it hurts to move like this. Emily moves to comfort him. Now she is pat pat patting him. Together we sit on the sofa.

"Let's not tell Sarah for a while, okay?" Father says.

The sun starts to set, and the room where we all are

grows dim. Jackson comes to the door and says that everyone's hungry. Mother Claire says soon, they'll eat soon.

When the door closes behind him, I say, "We could all go." My words are low to the floor. But they rise up some, float around our ankles. "All of us, Father. The whole family. We could leave."

The words move up up up until everyone hears them. Something close to excitement flitters in my chest. "I know we could make it, if it was all of us. All of us, Father. We could go. Run in the middle of the night."

Mother Claire glances at Father. Maybe . . . Mother Victoria is openmouthed again. They look at one another, back and forth. Have they thought this themselves? Will they leave this place?

"Where would a family like ours live?" Father's voice sounds heavy. He doesn't move, doesn't even blink for a long few moments. "It's God's will we stay," he says at last. He rubs his face, and for a moment I see him as an old man in this place with no way out. I crumple up inside.

Will I be an old woman here? The seventh wife to my uncle? The mother of my uncle's children?

We won't be leaving as a family. Father won't do it.

"They can't make me marry him," I say.

"They can," Father says.

Mothers Claire and Victoria nod. They believe it, too.

And for the first time I think, I think, they are right.

THERE ARE PEOPLE who *have* run from being a Chosen One. Some stayed in hiding for a long time. The God Squad looked for them. Sometimes they brought the people back, the women back. Sometimes a boy would get away.

Joshua and I, we were in hiding right here in front of everyone.

In the night. When it was late. When all were asleep. When the front gates were locked. That's when our hiding began.

We hid next to the community building where the women sometimes have quilting bees. Or on the far side of the building where there's a shadow so dark Joshua and I could stand still and not be noticed.

The back side of the Temple. In the basement stairwell.

Out behind my trailer.

Under his bedroom window.

Near the Fellowship Hall where people used to dance before and now we have barbecues each month to break two-day fasts.

Near the wild Russian Olive trees that make me sneeze every spring.

We hid every place we could.

Will Joshua be one of the boys who makes it?

And will he remember to come back and get me?

FOR FOUR DAYS I worry about Joshua. We bury Abigail. We finish my wedding dress. My mother cries about everything, visits her fourth dead baby's grave. The bruises on my face start to change color, from blue to a greenish yellow color.

At night, when I lie next to Laura, I think of Joshua. I imagine him coming back to my window. No! He comes to my front door. He says, "I've come for you, Kyra. I have a place for us. I'll bring you back to see your family all the time." Then he drives me away.

I'm not sure when I realize what's going to happen, but it comes to me like I've fallen flat on my face.

Joshua won't come.

I don't even know if he's alive. Not really.

I'm on my own. And in less than a week I'll be sharing my wedding bed with a man fifty years older than me.

IV

Only one thing makes me feel like I can make it.

It's books. Reading. I have to go back. Just one more time. If I can go to the Ironton County Mobile Library on Wheels one more time, smell the books, touch them, if I can do that, I think I'll make it. And at the same time I can tell Patrick not to come back, ever. "Just drive on past here," that's what I'll say. "Just drive on past here, Patrick, and don't stop, no matter if I stand in front of the van. You just keep going."

Knowing I'm going to say all this makes me feel better.

Makes me feel all right about visiting Patrick one more time.

The facts are these: They know I wander.

And Sheriff Felix has stopped Patrick at least once.

I always walk. And maybe now, it would be strange if I didn't *keep* walking.

But they are watching. They are all watching now. My brothers and sisters. My father and mothers. Only Mother Sarah, who keeps weeping, only she doesn't seem to notice me. She is gone off in her head, I think. To a place baby Abigail would live? I don't know.

But when Wednesday morning dawns, I am so itchy to get to the Ironton County Mobile Library on Wheels I have to scratch at my arms. My heart seems to be working double time. Pounding extra. I'm afraid and I have hours before anything will happen.

If I go walking.

Like I always have.

Even though they are watching.

At last I choose to go.

Thank goodness, thank goodness I have this last Wednesday to see Patrick at the Ironton County Mobile Library on Wheels and tell him, "Don't come back. This is me just telling you good-bye. Good-bye and thank you."

Just thinking the words makes a lump come up in my throat.

As I walk past the Temple toward the chain-link fence, I wonder if I should have shared this with Laura. The sun is hot. I've kept two secrets from her. Both secrets about men: Joshua and Patrick.

"But secrets will keep her safe," I say to myself as I edge my way out of the Compound.

The God Squad sees me go. From the corner of my eye, I watch them watch me.

But I always *go,* I think. Always.

I don't run. I act bored. I act the way I always act. Right?

Can they see my heart beating?

Can they smell my sweat?

I look behind me over and over as I walk away.

No one follows. Not one person. At last I can breathe air that isn't coming between clenched teeth.

It's when I'm waiting for the van of books to come pulling up—hoping Patrick will come, but maybe, maybe he won't—that panic sets in. Maybe he won't maybe he won't come by here again maybe because he was stopped once before and Sheriff Felix is scary maybe he has come by and I missed him and I should be home working on the veil for the ceremony The veil that will shield my face from Uncle Hyrum when we are married maybe he has been by and why should he stop now I wouldn't if I saw Sheriff Felix and he did and everyone is watching me they all are.

I wait, in the shade of the Russian Olive trees. I wait, just in case. And I decide right then, I can still read. Even if I am married.

I can read.

Women can read.

Their husbands don't have to know. I could do it in between all the other things a youngest wife has to do, including being available to her husband in case he wants her, because I cannot get to heaven if I don't have babies.

A young mother can read. If she wants it bad enough.

I could, I think in the shade, watching first one way down the road and then the other, *I could read to my babies.* No one would know. Uncle Hyrum is an Apostle. He might be gone a lot. He'd never know.

I could go to my trees. I could say I'm visiting my mother. I could walk right out here, if I wanted. I could.

An even better idea comes to me. Why, I could memorize the books. Just come to the Ironton County Mobile Library on Wheels once a week and write out a few pages of *Hop on Pop* or *Go, Dog. Go!* I could do that. I could. And then whisper the words in my babies' ears.

"You are crazy, Kyra Leigh Carlson," I say right out loud and that's when I see him. Coming from a distance. That big van, lumbering toward me. There's the Big Gulp cup on the dashboard. The fans are working, turning, and the closer the Ironton County Mobile Library on Wheels gets to me, the more my heart throbs, like it's squeezing in on itself.

"I won't stop coming here," I say to the wind. It's picked up some. I can feel it blowing, carrying bits of sand. "Just because I'm married doesn't mean that I can't check out books. And I *could* memorize things. Or I *could* hide the books and . . ."

There are tears in my eyes as I climb the van's stairs.

"Kyra," Patrick says when he sees my face. "What happened to you? Oh my gosh, what happened to you?"

And without a thought to how I shouldn't, I tell Patrick everything. Everything.

About The Chosen and Joshua and about Abigail coming too early because I got Mother Sarah so upset. I tell him everything. Standing on the steps, I start, then on the inside of the van. I lower myself to the floor. Words pour from me like water from a spigot, I speak that fast. So fast the words seem like they are all one. I'm not even sure he understands it all.

Patrick listens, crouching next to me.

I tell him all of it. Uncle Hyrum and those who have run and Ellen and the dead twins and my marriage and the beating. All around me are the smells of fresh newspapers and books. There is Patrick's smell, something sweet.

"I cannot believe this," he says after a moment. "This is un-freaking-believable. They beat the hell out of you."

What can I say to that?

Instead, he speaks again. And when he says it, the words are almost not there. "I'll take you with me."

179

I look at Patrick.

He's squatting there next to me, his economics book on the floor, that Big Gulp cup sweating.

"Right now," he says. "We'll get help. You can stay with my wife, Emily, and me. We'll do what we have to, Kyra. If you want."

He moves to his seat, waits for my answer, his hand hovers above the ignition.

I nod.

He starts the van, shifts into gear, and we are off.

AT THE SOUND of the engine, I start to cry. It's like my life flashes before my eyes. I see Laura, Margaret, and Carolina. I think of Father and Mother Sarah, empty of a baby and with me gone, no one to take care of her.

The tears fall warm on my hands as I look into my lap.

I'm still on the floor, right near the W section of this mobile library.

"It's okay, Kyra," Patrick says. "Everything's going to be okay. I promise." He turns his head. Looks at me briefly over his shoulder. Drives on.

The back of the Ironton County Mobile Library on Wheels sways and I am rocked against books. I pull my

180

knees under my chin, missing my family more than I thought possible.

I've left my music behind. And my sisters. And mothers. And father.

And Uncle Hyrum, a voice says.

I squeeze my eyes shut.

What will happen now?

When I don't go back home, what will happen? When will they notice? When will they see I am gone? Will the God Squad see me not come home? What will Mother Sarah do? Will she look for me, holding her stomach where Abigail used to be? Will Mother Claire and Mother Victoria go out with Father, walk the perimeter of the Compound, check the irrigation ditches?

What will Uncle Hyrum do?

Will Laura miss me? Margaret and Carolina? Will they miss me? What about Emily? Will she be okay if I'm gone? And Mariah?

How long before the Prophet sends someone to look for me?

"Stay down until we go past where you live," Patrick says. He flips on music and rocks his head in time. Then he says, "We're past. Give me a mile or so more."

I bounce a bit on the van floor. This bookmobile drives a lot more rough than our old van.

I'm so sad I can't even look at book titles. I'm so sad I think my heart may never be okay again.

Is getting away from Uncle Hyrum worth leaving my family for?

Don't think about home right now, the voice says. *Just get away.*

Patrick's voice interrupts my thoughts. "You want to come sit up here with me, Kyra?" He nods at the passenger seat as we drive away from my family. My family and Uncle Hyrum.

I'm still sniffling, but I say I will.

I make my way to the front of the van, swaying with the movement.

"It'll be okay, Kyra," Patrick says. I look him right in the eyes. I see he believes it.

Outside, flat land rolls past.

"I miss them already," I say and burst into fresh tears. "I'm never going to be allowed to see them again."

I know this is the truth as soon as I say it.

Laura will sleep alone from now on.

I won't scrooch up next to her.

I won't hold Mariah.

Again, Patrick reaches over and pats me. This time he pats my arm, right on a bruise, but I don't tell him so. The movement is awkward. Nothing like Father with me. Nothing like the way Mother loves me. Or Emily. But Patrick is sincere. And I have to believe in his sincerity. Maybe it will save my life.

WE HAVEN'T GOTTEN even fifteen miles from the Compound when Patrick says, "What? I wasn't breaking the speed limit." He taps at the brakes.

I look out the sideview mirror.

A police car is behind us and has its lights on.

All the sudden I am so full of energy, I could run faster than we're driving. "Don't stop," I say, my voice high and loud. "Patrick, don't stop."

"Why not?" he asks, still slowing the van. "It's a cop."

"No!" My voice doesn't sound like it belongs to me. "He's from the Compound. You cannot stop."

Patrick's face goes all funny. He says, "Is your seat belt on, Kyra?"

"Yes." I'm having trouble breathing.

I clutch the arms of the seat. The van bounces down the old road. Patrick slams the gas pedal all the way to the floor. He doesn't even slow down for potholes now.

Behind us a siren goes on. I can see the flash of the lights in the mirror.

"Oh no oh no," I say. "Oh no."

We race, and I know, like I know I may never see my

family again, that we're racing for our lives. The scenery flies past. I've never gone this fast before. Not ever. Not when I've driven with my mothers or when I've driven by myself. The sage and fencing seem like a blur.

The police car drives up next to us. I see Sheriff Felix in the front. He motions with his gun for us to pull over.

I scream so loud I hurt my own ears.

"Damn it," Patrick says. "This old thing won't go faster than seventy-five."

We hit a large hole and books smack onto the carpeted floor behind me. Patrick's Big Gulp drink trembles in the cup holder.

"There's someone else," Patrick says. He clutches the steering wheel. His knuckles are white. His face has lost all color. I can tell he's scared.

I'm scared. I am so scared I think I might throw up.

Again I look out the back in the mirror. As soon as I see the black Hummers, I know we're doomed.

"This is kidnapping," Sheriff Felix says through a loudspeaker. "Pull over."

"We just have to make it to the Ironton County line," Patrick says. Only he says it like he's been running for miles, not driving.

The police car pulls in front of us, and slows down. A Hummer moves in on the side, and one closes in at the back.

"Hold on, Kyra," Patrick says. "I'm not slowing down."

And as if to prove it, the van hits the back of Sheriff Felix's car.

"Ohnoohnoohno," I say. And then I start praying out loud. "Dear God, help us. Help us. Keep us safe. Help us. Please, God."

A car from behind rams the van. My head snaps forward, the seat belt catching me before I'm thrown into the dashboard.

"Amen," Patrick says.

"Please, God, please. I'm sorry. Help us. Please."

"Kyra," Patrick says. "Get my cell phone."

With his head he nods to the glove compartment. I open it. There it is. A slim black phone. "Not too much farther up the road and we'll get service," he says. "Turn it on now. When we get close enough, the phone will make a *chirrup* sound. The face will light up. Then you call nine-one-one."

"All right," I say.

I press the On button. My hands shake as I watch the cell phone.

There's no service at all.

"Just a little farther, baby," Patrick says to the Ironton County Mobile Library on Wheels.

"Come on, baby," I say.

A Hummer slams into the side of the van.

We swerve. More books fall from the shelves. The Big Gulp cup topples, splashing soda on my dress and legs.

I squeeze my eyes shut. "Oh God. Dearest Father. Please help us. Please get us to safety." My hands are clenched so tight I feel my nails cutting into my palms. My shoulder belt presses against my ribs and it hurts.

The Hummer hits us again. The picture of Emily and Nathan flutters to the floor.

Patrick slams on the brakes and the car behind us hits us. We swerve, running off the road. Back on. Dust billows. My mouth won't close. A small sound escapes me. The car comes to a halt next to a ditch and the van teeters. And then slides into the hole. Books scatter everywhere. Patrick and I are trapped. And there's still no service on the phone.

Patrick is suspended above me, his seat belt holding him. He kicks himself free. I'm lying on the door. He's bleeding. Blood drips down his chin, splats on my face and on the window next to me.

"Sorry," he says. And then, "Hide that phone. Run when they get us out of here, Kyra. And there's an extra key in the Ks."

"What?"

Patrick doesn't answer and I only have a chance to tuck the phone away.

Then they have us both out. On our knees. Hands locked behind us. Heads bent. In the sun of the late afternoon.

BROTHER FELIX TAKES ME away in the police car. I watch Patrick as we leave. I see them kick him over and over. I see him fall to the side. One of the God Squad pulls Patrick to his knees again.

My screaming won't stop. Not even when the sheriff hits me in the mouth, resplitting my lips. I taste blood. But I can't stop watching Patrick, who goes in and out of view because of the dust we've kicked up. I watch and scream his name.

Watch as they circle him.

I watch until I can't see him anymore.

What have I done?

More blood on my hands?

Dear God. What have I done?

"HE'S A PROPHET, you know that, don't you?"

I won't look at Sheriff Felix. I refuse to look at him. Don't look, just ignore him, I hate him, I hate his guts.

Instead, I stare out the window where Patrick was before. My eyes strain to see past the nothing that is there.

We've gone too far for me to see him. We're headed back. Headed back.

I look and imagine that he's there.

He's fine, Patrick is fine. I see him getting up, standing, fighting his way free. I keep my eyes looking to where he might be. He's in the Ironton County Mobile Library on Wheels, tipping it back on the tires. He's driving to save me.

"You hear me, Kyra?" Brother Felix says.

"I hear you," I say.

"I got a testimony of him," Brother Felix says. And his voice goes foggy with emotion.

Now I look at the police officer.

He glances at me, and I see his eyes have filled with tears.

"I know he rules. That he stands beside Jesus in power."

I say nothing, just listen.

"I'd do anything to serve him," he says. "I love him."

Behind me, what's happening?

I close my ears to Brother Felix.

Then I close my eyes.

After a moment, I pray again.

Dear God. Dear God. Please help him. Dear God, please don't let this prayer be too late. Please keep him safe. Please, for Nathan. For his Emily. For me.

———

THEY DO NOTHING to me.

Nothing.

Just send me home to Father and say, "Watch her."

Mother Claire comes to me later. "Don't try it again, Kyra," she says. She's wringing her hands. She never does that. "They've beaten you once. I'm surprised they didn't beat you when they got you back." She bites at her bottom lip. "Honey," she says, "I have a really bad feeling. A *really* bad feeling. Promise me you won't do it again."

Her words scare the spit out of me. I mean I cannot even work up enough moisture to wet my tongue. I can't answer her.

All I have in my head is Patrick. What happened to Patrick?

The next day, as soon as I see the Ironton County Mobile Library on Wheels van hidden near my stand of Russian Olives, like they're trying to cover it but not, I know something is bad wrong.

The hairs rise on my neck. I slow my walk, pretending not to look, but looking anyway.

And then here comes the God Squad. Stepping out of the shadows the van makes. Two of Prophet Childs's bodyguards. They're big. I see them see me pretending I don't see the van.

They watch me walk. Brother Nelson raises his sunglasses so I can see his eyes. He moves his head in a gesture like he's saying, "You."

They've parked it here on purpose. Where I can see it. To show me. So I know. Without saying a word they're telling me to behave, to do what I'm told. Or else. Or else whatever they've done to Patrick, they'll do to me.

I keep my walk steady, though I want to run back to my trees. Or run to the van. Search for Patrick. My lips have gone numb. I'm dizzy. My hands feel like they're asleep.

I feel sick to my stomach. I'm going to throw up. Right here. Right now. Right in my yard with them watching me pretending not to see anything.

But I can't vomit.

I have to just go on back in the house. Just go on back. With that cell phone that won't even work tucked in my dress like I used to tuck Patrick's books. Acting like I don't know anything.

Oh, but I do.

I do.

I know, without seeing the body, that Patrick is dead.

WHEN THEY ARE GONE, as evening sets in, I sneak over to the van and peer in the window. The books are still spilled, all over the back on the floor. They didn't throw away Patrick's Big Gulp cup. It's crushed on the passenger's side of the van. Did I step on it after it fell? I don't remember.

They didn't even clean the blood out of the van. I see it spattered all over the windshield, gone brown. On the seat. In a puddle on the carpet. Pooled and dried and cracking on the floor.

It's Patrick's blood, I know.

Did they kill him in here? Where's his body?

Somehow, I make it over to my Russian Olive tree and climb as high as I am able. Straight up into the branches. Into the thorns. Even when I am stabbed, I don't care.

My friend is dead.

I cry with my mouth open, but I don't make a sound. Not a sound. I cry until I'm gasping for breath, and once, I almost fall from my tree. I cry until I am hoarse, even though I've not made one bit of noise.

My family calls for me in hushed tones, "Kyra. Kyra, come home."

I don't. I stay in the tree and cry.

Poor Nathan. Poor Emily. Waiting for Patrick to come home. I cry until the moon is high in the sky.

Then I go back home.

I crawl into bed beside Laura. That is when I realize, lying next to my sister, that I am not me anymore.

I'm not sure who I am. Mother Claire and Father and dead Abigail and Emily and Laura and Joshua and music and Patrick and books and death—no, murder!—it all has changed me. If I looked into the mirror, I am pretty sure that everything about me, under the bruises and cuts, would be changed. I would *not* have the same eyes. Would *not* have the same face shape. Would *not* have the same hair color.

I am not me anymore.

I go to sleep knowing that.

I am not me. Any. More.

I HAVE NO IDEA what time I wake up. It might be ten minutes after I went to sleep, it might be almost morning. One thing I know is that I am still changed. I am not me, still. I think I've grown hollow.

In the semidarkness I see my wedding dress hanging from a coat hanger on the closet door. It's like a ghost.

Quiet, I get out of bed and go looking for Mother's sewing scissors. On the living-room floor, where Mother laid out the fabric before Abigail died, I cut the wedding dress into strips. Thin strips. Too thin for even a quilt. So thin you could only start a fire.

"Kyra?" Laura stands in the doorway of our room.

I start. My hands are full of fabric. I see I've dropped some of it. It's there on the floor, at Laura's feet.

"What are you doing?"

When I open my mouth, no words come out at first. There! Now Laura will see my change. She'll see I'm different. How does she recognize me? At last I say, "I'm leaving."

She pads across the floor, puts her arms around me and the strips of fabric. Presses her lips to my face.

"Where are you going?" Her breath is warm and I close my eyes.

"Away from here," I say because the changed me doesn't care where. Just out. Just get out.

When I look at her, there are tears on Laura's face. "Don't go," she says. But she kisses me good-bye. Again and again.

"I love you," she says.

"I love you, too," I say.

She stands on the porch and watches me walk away. Her voice follows me into the near darkness. "Good-bye, my Kyra." Her voice tells me she's still crying.

I stop off at Uncle Hyrum's place. Spread the fabric all over the steps, all over the bushes near the front, on the lush grass of his yard. If he hadn't wanted to marry me, I wouldn't be leaving. If he hadn't wanted me, Joshua might still be here. Baby Abigail would be alive. Patrick would be alive.

But no, that's not completely right.

This all goes past Uncle Hyrum.

It's not *just* his fault. Maybe not his fault at all.

I stop and squeeze my hands tight, then start back

193

toward my Russian Olive trees. Mother and Father believe. They believe they are doing right. I am sure of this.

Or I was before I changed.

THE DOOR TO THE Ironton County Mobile Library on Wheels opens without even a noise. I pull it shut behind me, but not quite all the way. Then I untuck Patrick's cell phone from where I'd hidden it in my dress and turn it on. My hands shake like crazy.

No service. That's what it says. I look back at the spilled books.

There's an extra key in the Ks. He said that. Patrick said it. A key to the van, I'm sure.

It's hard to walk in the almost dark, through all these novels. Do I step on stories I've read? Is that first book, *Bridge to Terabithia,* in this mound?

A few books move under my foot and I slip to one knee. I crawl to where the Ks are. The shelf is near the ground.

Using the cell phone as light, I pull the titles out and stack them into a neat pile. Dick King-Smith, Gordon Korman, Uma Krishnaswami. And then there it is. Taped to the shelf. A key.

It's cool and a little sticky in my hand. I crawl back over the books and climb into the driver's seat. Into Patrick's seat.

I put the phone in the cup holder where those Big Gulp cups sat.

I squeeze my eyes shut. "Just get to cell-phone service," I whisper. The shaking has moved from my hands to my knees. It's like my legs have no bone.

Outside, it's dark enough that if I didn't know this Compound like my own sisters' faces, I would be in trouble.

"Oh, you're in trouble, all right," I say. The new me almost smiles. I ease the van into neutral.

The Ironton County Mobile Library on Wheels, banged up and dented all around, starts the first time I turn the key. The sound is like a bomb going off to my ears. Hopefully I'm far enough away from the God Squad that I'll have some time.

I put the van into drive. It lurches almost from under me and I slam on the brakes, jerking forward in the seat. "You've driven with Mother," I say. Then I grasp the wheel with all my power and hold on for dear life. For my own dear life.

"You can do this, Kyra Leigh Carlson. You can."

You have to, I think.

Thank goodness they parked the van here, so close to my home. There's no fencing this side of my home, just at the front of the Compound. I creep along. Afraid to go too fast. I steer near the trailer. Laura is on the steps, waiting. She watches as I drive past her and I think my heart might give me up right this second. I look as hard as I can at her, hard as

I can as I drive away. Put my hand on the window. And she watches me, too. Standing there. My sister. Her hand raised to me. I think we can almost touch.

Then she is gone. And I move away from my home, my father's trailers. My brothers and sister. My mothers.

I ease the van past everyone's property, behind gardens but near to fields, going so slow, my foot shaking on the gas pedal. With a gasp I suck in air, realizing I haven't been breathing. Now—it seems an eternity—now I drive past the fence and turn the direction I went with my mothers just a few days ago. The direction I went with Patrick, poor Patrick, yesterday.

Still I am cautious. Still I am slow. Hoping this engine makes no sound. Hoping no one but Laura knows I'm gone. Hands shaking, my knees weak. I pull out on the road and when I think no one can hear this old bookmobile, I push the pedal down and I am free, going forty-five miles per hour. Away.

"DID YOU THINK you would get free without a fight?" That's what I say to myself when I see the headlights come up on the road behind me.

"As if I wasn't shaking enough before," I say to the blood on the window.

This is as close as I'm getting to Patrick. Talking to his blood.

In the rearview mirror I see the car lights blink off and on.

"I'm not pulling over," I say.

I don't speed up at all. Just keep the Ironton County Mobile Library on Wheels going at that easy forty-five miles per hour.

"You realize," I say to what is left of Patrick, "that they'll kill me, too."

The Hummer pulls up to the side window. They snap on the interior light. I can't quite look at them. I'll wreck sure. When I ease up on the gas, my leg jumps, I'm so scared. I can just see Brother Laramie in the passenger seat. He points to the side of the road, making his finger like a gun.

"All you have to do," Patrick says in my head, "is get to the Ironton County line. We were almost there before. We almost made it."

"I can do that," I say. "I'm not so good at driving, but I can get there."

"Just get to service for the phone. Then dial nine-one-one."

If you're there, God, I think, *please help me.* But He didn't help Patrick, did He?

"You only have a few more miles to go." Patrick's voice is like a whisper in my brain.

In the bed of the Ironton County Mobile Library on

Wheels, I can hear books sliding this way and that as I drive along this pot-holed road. My hands are clenched so tight they feel frozen. And in my head, right behind Patrick's voice, there is a small pain, growing.

"Is that where they'll shoot me?" I say.

"You'll be fine," Patrick says. "Just fine."

Beside me, Brother Laramie has rolled down the window. He calls out. "Kyra," he says. "Sister Carlson."

I refuse to look at him.

"Patrick?" I say. "Patrick?"

"Pull on over, girl," Brother Laramie says. "You don't have much gas."

He's right. I can see that on the control panel. Looking down causes me to almost hit the God Squad's car. They drop back some.

"Slow and steady wins the race." This is Mother Sarah's voice. Telling me the tortoise and the hare story. In my head I see her standing near to Patrick. And then there's Father.

"Run, Kyra. Get out of here. Get free." His voice is as soft as the other two, but the words are more urgent.

"I'm trying, Father," I say, gripping the steering wheel.

I speed the van up. Go a little faster. In the distance I can see the sun turning the sky a clear blue.

"Drive to town," says Joshua.

Joshua's here!

"I am," I say.

I'm nowhere near where they stopped us before, where they stopped Patrick and me before, when the phone lets out a little singsong sound. I see it there in the cup holder, all lit up.

"It can't be," I say.

"Pull over, Kyra," someone yells out at me.

But that is all the time I have for them in the car next to me.

I'm careful when I dial. Careful when I push the speaker button on the phone. Careful when I set the phone back into the Big Gulp cup holder.

"This is nine-one-one. What's your emergency?"

"I'm running away," I say.

"Please speak louder."

Under my hands, the steering wheel shakes as I drive over the washboard dirt road.

"Stop the vehicle now."

I glance at Brother Laramie. I can just see Brother Nelson. And a gun. He has a gun!

"Help me." My voice is loud.

I don't want to die.

(Patrick didn't want to die either. He had a wife and a son.)

"They have a gun," I say. "They have a gun." Will I get this far and follow Patrick?

"Where are you?"

I tell the woman that I'm heading toward town. What I am driving.

"You're in a mobile book van?" she says.

Brother Laramie points to the side of the road with the gun.

I pretend like he's not there.

"They've killed people already," I say. I tell her Patrick's name. Give them Ellen's name, too, though they wouldn't know her. "If I stop, they'll kill me. I know it."

"I'm sending help," the woman says. "We have an officer in the area."

Out here? Out here in the middle of nowhere?

"Keep talking to me," she says.

I'm not sure if I can drive faster and talk at the same time, but I push the van forward. The light on the control panel comes on with a ding, letting me know I am almost out of gas.

"Who are you?" the operator asks.

I can't say anything. Just hold the wheel.

"Kyra," Patrick says in my head. "Tell her that. Tell her where you live."

"The Chosen Ones," I say. "I'm part of The Chosen Ones." It sounds like my voice is trying to escape from me.

She talks to someone else, calling for backup.

The Hummer keeps pace beside me.

Tears splash down my face. I didn't even realize I was crying.

My hands hurt.

The pain in my head, the place where they'll shoot me if I stop, intensifies.

Brother Laramie sticks the gun out the window. He fires at the back of the Ironton County Mobile Library on Wheels. I hear the bullet rip through metal. I scream.

"Hold on," the operator says. "Hold on. I have someone coming for you."

And just as she says it, I see flashing lights headed in my direction.

THE POLICE CARS, two, three, four of them, roar past and stop Brother Felix, who is in his police cruiser (how did I miss him back there?), and both Hummers that followed me. They are all stopped, pulled out of their cars, and while I'm watching, handcuffed.

I'm swept to a police car where a woman officer looks so angry when she sees my face that she makes her partner wait before they talk to me.

"You're not going back there, O'Neil," the man cop says.

"The hell I'm not," she says. "I'm sick of what this community is doing to these children."

I watch her march in the morning sun, her shadow falling long on the road beside her. She is so angry I think she'll walk right through Brother Felix. She yells in his face, just inches from him. The other officers watch her. One of them is grinning.

She comes back, hand on her gun.

"Who are they?" she says to me. She's pulled on her sunglasses. They are little mirrors and when she turns to ask me this question, I see myself. Right there. Twin reflections. Me. *Me.*

"The God Squad," I say.

I move to the side of the police car, somehow getting to the sideview mirror. The lights flash. I see them go across my body.

"Honey?" Officer O'Neil says. She touches my shoulder. "What do you need?"

I look back at her, and there I am again, in her sunglasses. Two of *me.* I can't answer. I just stare at myself. It's *me* in the reflection. I haven't changed at all. Not at all. I touch my lips with my fingers, see the bruising in the morning light, see my mouth trying to heal. I can hear the radio crackling in the police car.

How can this be?

I was sure, sure, I had changed. Sure of it, that only the new me would run. That if I saw me, I would be different. Sure only the new me would have been able to get away. The hollow places inside me start to fill up.

"Honey," Officer O'Neil says, "come sit down." She points

to the backseat of the police car and I slip inside.

"What is it?" she says.

I look at her—look at *me*—and say, "I'm still here."

"What?" She raises the glasses. Her eyes are dark brown.

"I thought . . ." I'm not quite sure what I thought. "I thought they might have killed me, too."

With a gentle hand Officer O'Neil touches my face. "No, honey," she says. "You're safe now."

I TELL THE DETECTIVES all of it, every single bit, even though my heart feels like it will give out the way it pounds. I tell about the Lost Boys and Bill and Ellen. All about Patrick and the graves of the unwhole children. I tell them about the beatings and the book burnings and how the girls are saved for the old men. I talk and talk until my throat burns when I sip down the orange juice they give me. I talk through tears and sometimes I'm so angry my head hurts.

After I tell them what I know, the police say I'll be going to a safe house.

"A safe house?" I say to Officer O'Neil as we head off. I remember Joshua saying something about a safe house. Will he be there? It's dusk and the streets are full of cars, the sidewalks full of people. Are they headed to their homes, all of them? Everything aches from my crying and talking and crying and talking.

Officer O'Neil looks at me, then she reaches for my hand.

"A place where you'll be safe, Kyra," she says. She clears her throat. "There's a warrant for Mark Childs and some of those other thugs."

By thugs she means the God Squad.

We're quiet a moment.

"The Chosen have come here before," she says, flipping on her blinker. We turn and chase the headlights down the road. "To Samantha Oberg's."

"What?"

"When polygamists run, we sometimes put them up in this house. At least for a day or two. Or until we can get them settled into the foster-care system."

"Oh." I look out the window. Foster care. Is that where Joshua ended up? Do the Lost Boys stay with this Samantha Oberg? We drive for a while. The radio in Officer O'Neil's car talks to her and to other people. I don't have to say anything.

The sky changes into an almost purple-blue. There are lots of houses lining the streets out here. Less city. More country, it seems. Some homes are big, some smaller. But nearly all of them have their lights on. The light falling out of the houses like that makes my heart hurt more. I miss my family. For a moment I see Laura in my mind, see her with her hand up as I drive away.

Officer O'Neil pulls into a driveway of a house that has a porch across the front and down both sides. A woman leans against the rail. A girl stands beside her. But there is no Joshua. No Joshua.

"That's Samantha," Officer O'Neil says. "We told her about you and she told me she couldn't wait to meet you."

She's to us before the engine is off. She wears a pair of blue jeans and a pink top. Her hair is pulled back in a pony-tail. At first I think she's in her early twenties until she stands at my car window. Then I can see she's older.

"I am so glad you're here, Kyra," she says when I step outside. Her face is full of smiles.

Officer O'Neil gets out of the car and hugs me good-bye. Tears fill my eyes. For a moment I'm not sure I won't follow her right back to the police station.

"I'll see you again," she says into my hair. "I'll check in on you."

"Okay." My voice is a whisper.

Samantha has hold of my hand in an instant. "Let's go inside." We walk toward the light and the house and the girl.

But I pull back. Turn to watch Officer O'Neil drive away. Then the cars that pass on the street close enough, it seems, I could reach out and touch them. I watch it all.

Less than fifty miles from here is my family. I can't quite move, can't quite breathe thinking of them without me.

A wind picks up and I smell something sweet. Roses maybe? Samantha touches my arm. "It's hard at first," she says. Her voice is low, like it rides the breeze.

I want to nod, let her know I hear her, but I can't.

"I did it myself, Kyra," she says.

I stare away.

"Not from The Chosen Ones, but from the Fundamentalists. I've been where you are now. I got the hell out of there." She laughs. Even though things aren't funny at all, she laughs. "I ran. And they followed me."

Now I look at her, straight in the eyes.

"I ran more than once. I was sixteen and married. I had a baby. Somehow I carried us both away."

I look at the girl on the porch. She's probably my age. The air is soft around my face.

"That's my second daughter, Madison," Samantha says. "The first is at the university."

We're both quiet. Then Samantha says, "I hear they followed you."

"Yes," I say.

My dress seems too tight around the wrists. She looks at me.

"And I see they gave you a good beating, too."

"Yes."

"Gotta keep you little ones in line, don't they? Or you could be dangerous."

I look back at where Officer O'Neil drove away.

"I bet you're starved," Samantha says. "Let's get something to eat, you want?"

"Can I go, too, Mom?" Madison has snuck up behind us. She wears blue jeans and a top with tiny sleeves. Her bra shows. I look away. I'll never wear anything that shows my bra. Never!

"Sure," Samantha says. She puts an arm around her daughter. "Let's go to IHOP."

.

IN THE CAR

In the restaurant

I wonder how I will fit in here. Outside. Away and with the sin of bras that show.

My hair, my bruises, the reminder of words not that long ago, *Polygamists, you can tell by their clothes,* all of it separates me and makes me different. People stare when we walk in and find a seat. Like before at Applebee's. But then I was with my mothers. Then I was with Laura.

Now I'm with strangers.

"Do you have brothers and sisters?" Madison asks. She's been looking at me from the side of her eye. Maybe she's

207

never seen anyone who's been beat up. At first, her looking, her sneaky stares, make me angry. But then her question, it knocks my anger aside.

"Yes," I say. "Lots of both." I pause. "And there are four girls with my mother." No, that's not right. "There were four girls. Now there are just three."

There should be five, a voice says, but I ignore it.

Madison nods. "I'm the baby." She scrunches her nose at me.

Mariah, too, the voice says.

"We have lots to do tomorrow," Samantha says. She sips a cup of hot chocolate topped with whipped cream. "We need to take you clothes shopping."

"Clothes?"

"You can't just wear *that*," Madison says. "You need something else. Something in style."

I keep my eyes on the turquoise tabletop. I don't say anything, but I think. I think, *Nothing that shows my bra like* some *people sitting here.*

The waitress sets our food in front of us. We all have the same thing—strawberry-stuffed crepes, hash browns, and tall mugs of hot chocolate. "Because you'll love it," Madison said when we ordered.

She's right, though I don't want her to be because of the dress comment. But the whipped cream and strawberries together are so good I think I might cry again. My mother would love this.

"And you can think about school, Kyra," Samantha says.

"You're my age," Madison says. She's taking huge bites of food. And I can tell this isn't such a treat for her as it is for me. "So you'd be with me. In eighth grade."

"You can think about it," Samantha says.

I eat, silent. And then, "I'd like to play a piano."

"Now?" Madison says.

Samantha says, "There's one at home. In the family room. I can show you tomorrow. Nothing spectacular. But it's in tune."

"Okay. What about a bookmobile?" For a moment, there's Patrick, grinning at me about a novel I've chosen. Showing me the newest book that he's put aside.

"A bookmobile?" Madison says, and Samantha says, "We have a great library in town."

My throat is tight with crepes and Patrick's memory.

"A library would be good," I say, and my voice is just a whisper.

LATE THAT NIGHT, I lie under the sheet in this new bed. My tummy is tight, it's so full.

"We're glad you're here, Kyra," Samantha says. "You've got a room with us as long as you need it. Good night." She leaves, closing the door. I hear her walk away, hear her as she tucks Madison into bed. They talk for a few minutes. Are they talking about me?

Their murmuring voices remind me of my home. I wonder at my family. Do they miss me? Do they want me back home? Do I want to *go* back home?

Yes! Yes, I do!

There's a tap at the door.

"What?" I sit up, the new nightgown Samantha pulled from a package for me itching at the back of my neck.

She leans into this room again. "Can I come in, Kyra?" The soft light from down the hall breaks all around her.

I nod, then say, "Yes."

She settles on the side of my bed. Light comes into my room fat as a slice of pie. I feel, all the sudden, heavy with grief.

"Look," Samantha says. She takes in a deep breath. "This isn't going to be easy for you. It's not, Kyra. But—" She pulls in more air. Clasps her hands in front of her. "But it's going to be worth it. In the long run."

I can't even move.

"I missed my family like crazy, after I ran. But not my husband. Or my sister wives. I had my Jessica when I left, so I wasn't entirely alone."

Like me, I think.

"But if you hang in there, you'll be okay. I just wanted you to know that."

"Okay." I'm not sure she even hears me.

She sits quiet and then says, "I've never had anyone stay longer than a month, but maybe that can change, Kyra. If you want."

"Maybe," I say.

THE IRONTON COUNTY Mobile Library on Wheels rolls down the road. I sit beside Patrick, a stack of books on my lap, a Big Gulp cup balanced on top. Laura is in the back of the van, picking books up and putting them on the shelves.

"Hold those steady, Kyra," Patrick says. "Hold them steady. You are gonna love what I picked out for you to read."

Laura says, "The God Squad are behind us."

I look out the window. Everything is in black and white, like all the color has been washed from the world.

"Hurry, Patrick, hurry." The books rock on my lap.

Patrick guns the engine, and just like that we take off into the sky, straight toward heaven. Fast! The God Squad grow small, like ants, on the road below.

"They'll never get us here," I say.

"That's right," Laura says.

"You're safe, Kyra," Patrick says.

I AWAKE with a start.

"Patrick?"

Outside, the wind blows.

I listen for the God Squad. For Patrick. There are tapping noises at my window.

"Laura?" I say. "Laura?"

It takes me a moment to figure out where I am.

"Laura's not here," I say into the darkness.

The sound at the window continues. And that's when I know, I *know,* that Joshua is out there. That *he's* come for me.

I throw back the covers and hurry to the window. I open the curtains.

There is no Joshua, just a tree. The branches scratch on the windowpane.

"You knew he couldn't be here," I say.

And I did, but still I start to cry. Not just because there's no Joshua but because there's no Laura or Margaret or Carolina. There's no Mariah or Mother Sarah or Father. There's no family waiting outside the window for me.

I crumple to the floor and weep. Who would think I could cry as much as I have today? But all that crying lets something loose in my brain.

Yes, my brain tells me, this is going to be hard. Like Samantha said. It's going to be awful, living away from what I know. Without my family.

But look what Patrick did. And Joshua, too.

I am free.

(No old man waiting for me.)

If I want, I can look for Joshua. Find him.

I am free.

Thin morning light seeps into my window through the leaves of the tree when, at last, I crawl back into bed. And just as I let my eyes close, I realize that it's a Russian Olive outside, tapping at my window.

Turn the page for an excerpt from
Carol Lynch Williams's new novel

Miles from
Ordinary

AVAILABLE WINTER 2011

I

There are mice.

Lots of mice. Running all over my room. Letting out crying sounds that grate on my ears. They crawl on my feet. I feel them on my arms. Soft things with toenails like blunt needles.

"Momma?" I say. She's dressed in a long nightgown. Her fingernails are sharp like the tops of just-opened cans. "We gotta get rid of the mice. We gotta call an exterminator." I hand her an old-fashioned phone.

"You're right, Lacey," Momma says. But instead of calling,

she cuts at her face with her nails. Deep wounds open up, split wide, and blood, dark blood like ink, makes paths down her face to the floor. She cries.

"Stop that," I say. "Stop it now."

But Momma doesn't listen. Just cuts and cries.

I AWOKE WITH A START, my heart thudding in my neck. My whole body felt like I'd been dunked in an ice bath.

"Only a dream," I said to myself. Then glanced at the clock. 3:46. I started to close my eyes. The wind nudged at the house. I could smell the magnolia tree.

Something moved in the corner.

"Hello?" I said, clutching my sheet to my chest. "Someone here?"

There was no answer.

The floor creaked near the closet.

"Hello?" I said. I wanted to sit up in bed, but I couldn't quite move. "Granddaddy?" My voice came out small. It felt like all the hair on my head was trying to get away from me.

"Lacey?"

Fear flashed a white streak behind my eyes. I gave a jump. "Granddaddy?"

"Lacey?"

Momma! It was Momma! Calling a second time from

her room. Her voice sad and scared and weepy. So the crying part of my dream was real. And maybe there was a mouse near the closet. A mouse coming from my dreams, alive and real? That was ridiculous. Of course that couldn't be.

"Are you okay?" I called to Momma. I kept my eyes toward the closet. Straining to see. Just darkness. No movement now.

The night breeze pushed into my room. The smell of the ocean. So peaceful. No more sounds from the closet. Good. Good. I took in a breath to push my fear away.

"Granddaddy," I said, hoping he wasn't close enough to hear me, "this is *my* room." A girl should at least have privacy in her bedroom. My heartbeat slowed.

"Lacey? I need you."

Momma.

"Coming."

Man, was I tired. My eyes burned. But I threw my feet over the side of the bed. As soon as I touched the cool wood of the floor, fear surged in behind me. Run! I hurried toward my mother's room. It was like something chased me down the hall though I knew . . . *Did I* . . . there was nothing there.

A few more steps *Go, go!* and I made it. "What is it, Momma?" I leaned against the doorjamb. Her nightlight showed the pattern of flowers on the carpet.

"I'm scared." Her voice was shaky. Did she have a nightmare, too? "Granddaddy keeps bothering me. Has he been coming into your room? I've told him not to. To let you sleep because of tomorrow." Momma's voice wasn't even as loud as a whisper. I had to walk to the side of her bed to hear. I could just see her slender form under the blankets. "And I told him *I* have to sleep, too, because of you-know-what."

I nodded but Momma didn't look my way. Just gripped the sheet and blanket in her fingers and spoke like maybe I was glued to the ceiling.

"But he won't let me alone," Momma said. She glanced at me, then back again. "If you get in bed with me, Lacey, I think he'll stay outta here for awhile."

Had he been to my room? For a moment I felt something behind me. Like someone watched. The feeling was muddy, heavy. Almost on my shoulder. Almost pushing me toward Momma. I refused to look back. Not that I could have seen much of anything. The darkness was fat, almost difficult, in the hall.

"Will you sleep with me?"

"All right, Momma." Forcing myself not to hurry, *Quick, move it!* I took my time. Granddaddy might be the boss of this house, but I wasn't going to let him know he scared me, too. I climbed in next to my mother and snuggled her up. "Turn on your side and I'll scrooch up to your back."

"Okay, Lacey. Okay."

Momma was so thin I could feel her ribs. Could have

220

counted them. I could smell her sweat, too. "You go on to sleep," I said. "If Granddaddy comes back in, I'll send him out."

Don't let him come in here. And then, *You know he won't.* And another, *He could.*

"Thank you, baby," Momma said. "You watch for him awhile. But wake me if he tries anything."

I yawned big. "I will." Here I was, all of thirteen years old, and I was crawling into bed with my momma.

You big scaredy cat, I thought. *Don't let him come in here. You know he won't. He can't. Not possible.*

With Momma so close, my fears faded some. My heart slowed. And at last I was asleep.

II

At *10:32* A.M., I moved away from Momma's sleeping body and eased myself outta bed. I sucked in at morning air, glad for daylight.

Today was to be a big occasion. Big for Momma.*and* me. Both the Peace City Library and the Winn Dixie grocery store had a nice surprise waiting for them. Us! *We* were headed their way to start our new jobs.

Please, please, please.

Into my room I went, walking on tiptoe, the hardwood

floor smooth under my feet. I glanced at my closet door, but it was closed tight.

"Just your old imagination, Lacey," I said, making my voice loud enough anyone listening in would hear me. "So get on with the day."

Before bed last night, I'd pulled out my clothes: a dark blue shirt that Momma said looks real nice with my eyes, and a pair of tan shorts.

Now I was so excited I felt a little sick. This was something I had waited for a long time. I gazed at myself in the dresser mirror, pushing back my hair. My face looked okay, a little wrinkled on one side where the pillow had been bunched up under my head. But I didn't appear too tired. I'd slept most of the night. This time.

"Peace City Library," I said, almost smiling. "I'm a-coming."

Jumbled-up nerves made me feel like I could take off running fast as the hummingbirds flit from hibiscus flower to hibiscus flower in our side yard. That's how excited I was about my new job. And jittery, too.

"Lacey," I said, leaning close to my image and running a brush through my long, heavy hair. "This summer is gonna be okay." I thought for a moment. Closing my eyes and letting my imagination spring out with the good crazies. "Maybe," I said in a whisper, "maybe I'll meet a friend." Opening my eyes, I wiggled my head at my reflection. "A girlfriend. And she can . . ." I hesitated, then took in a breath ". . . and she can spend the night. And we can talk on the phone. Go to the mall maybe."

Nervousness and exhilaration ran out to the tips of my fingers. Anything could happen. Anything at all.

"Lacey," Momma called from her room. Her voice sounded weak. My stomach dropped a little. "Where are you?"

"Getting dressed. I'm coming." I opened my eyes extra wide but didn't move from in front of the mirror. I threw my nightshirt onto my bed, then slipped the shorts and top on. Flip-flops from under the bed *Don't look there* and I was ready to go.

"Is your granddaddy back?" Momma said.

I glanced at my closet. "No, he's not."

"Lacey, I need you to come talk to me." Her voice had gone whiney. Puny even. Still, her words were like Batman's Mr. Freeze. They stuck my feet to the floor. Cooled the blood in my veins. "I don't think I can go today."

"Oh yes you can," I said low so she wouldn't hear me. There was no way. No way would I let this happen. I plopped the brush onto the bed, my hair half done.

"Unthaw, girl," I said to myself. "Get going." In the mirror I could see two splotches of red on my cheeks. I turned fast and headed from my room toward Momma's. No arguments. Not now. I wanted out of here.

"You are in charge. This time, Lacey," I whispered to myself, "*you* are in charge of the day and this job. Just . . ." I could only think of *be strong*. But be strong was like a sit-com. Be strong was what people said right before the end of the show and everything turns out good.

"Don't worry, Momma," I said. "I can help you get dressed."

Now that I was defrosted, I hurried, quick, into Momma's room. It was dark and stuffy, the nightlight throwing a small yellow splash on a bit of the wall and the carpet, too. Those old flowers, plum colored and different looking in the day. Not that you would even know that the sun waited outside if this was the only room you went into.

I flicked on the overhead light and then the lamp next to Momma's bed. Sat down next to her.

"Now Momma," I said. Something like desperation tried to claw at me, but I wouldn't let it. Stomped it flat. Pushed it away. "Remember how we practiced? Remember how we rode the bus downtown? Stopped you in at the Winn Dixie and everything? Got the application. Filled it out. And they called you. You remember that?"

Momma looked at me, all dark-eyed from the bed. Her body almost not there under the covers. She gripped her blanket and nodded.

"You can do this. And you yourself said we're running outta money."

"I know," she said. She turned her head away from me. "If only there was more. If only I hadn't spent it all. But you know I had to, Lacey." She looked me in the eye. "I *had* to."

"I know it," I said. "I know it."

"For you," Momma said. "I have to keep you safe, Lacey." Momma dragged a breath in. Sometimes the way she breathed sounded like work. Like it was all she could do. "A mother's duty is to take care of her only child."

"I know that," I said. "And you going downtown? Well, that is like you taking care of me."

She nodded a little. Looked away again. Stared at the ceiling.

I reached out and took her hand. Her fingers were like little pencils. "The people at the Winn Dixie are waiting for you. They want *you* to work for them. They want to pay *you*. You're gonna do just fine."

Now Momma looked in my direction. Her face smudged from not sleeping. Her eyes almost empty. But after a moment, she gave me a little smile. "I'll do it," she said. It almost sounded like there was an energy to her voice. "I'll do it. For you. For duty."

I grinned at her, relief coming to take the place of the almost clawing. "And I'll get breakfast going while you dress."

Momma sat up and I squeezed her tight in a hug. "I sure do love you," I said, my words like feathers.

226

"And I love you, baby girl." She patted my back, thumping her hands on me like I was a drum. "You are such a help."

Before she could change her mind, I ran from the room and down the stairs to the kitchen.

"Granddaddy," I said, grabbing the makings for pancakes. There wasn't anyone in the room but me, so I spoke to the air, throwing my voice where he would hear me if he was near. "Granddaddy, don't be bothering my mother today. She needs to get away from here."

Soon as I said those words, I remembered Aunt Linda. Right before she left she'd said almost that same thing to Momma. "Angela," Aunt Linda had said, "you need to get away from this house. You need to get free of those memories."

Momma had watched Aunt Linda, quiet. It had been like a showdown, something from TV. The two of them standing there, squaring off, face to face, eye to eye. If it had been a show on television it would have been a Western, and one of them would have drawn a gun. Shot the other right down. Dead in the street.

"It's not good for you to stay here." Aunt Linda had brushed back the hair that fell into her face. Her cheeks were colored bright pink. It's hard to stand up to Momma, but she had. Yes, she had.

And Momma had said, "This is *my* place. Don't you forget

it. You hear me, Linda?" The words squeezed between her teeth. Shot into the air. Hit their target.

Momma had drawn the gun that day.

The thought of that fight still made me ache. And it was more than a year ago.

"Don't go there," I said, and started working on breakfast.

I had pancakes and eggs frying when Momma came down the stairs dressed for her first day of work. The window over the sink was cracked open an inch, and a morning breeze came in at us, freshening the room some, pushing pancake smell around. Momma's steps were slow and quiet—almost like a ghost. Outside green tree frogs called for rain.

"Close the window, Lacey." Momma flung her hand in a *get away* gesture, like the motion could shut out the air, close the window itself. "You know they can't be opened. Not a good thing. Too much comes in through openings like that."

"Right," I said, and pushed the glass shut.

"New day for both of us," Momma said. "How do I look?" She turned in a little circle to model her Winn Dixie apron. Her almost-black hair was swept up in a loose ponytail. I could see she was clean. *Good, good.*

"Whoo-eee!" I said. "Momma, there won't be a prettier checker in all the Winn Dixies in the whole wide world."

She gazed at me, big-eyed. Her voice got all soft. "You mean it?"

"I do."

She was quiet a moment, leaning onto the counter. Thinking right over the top of my head. "Your granddaddy? I bet he'd be proud of me this morning. Yes, Daddy would be proud." She straightened tall, then glanced over her shoulder, toward the stairs that entered the kitchen. "Wouldn't you, Daddy?"

There was no answer.

"Absolutely he would," I said, throwing a quick look in the same direction. "Starting a new job and all." Outside, the sun fell through the trees and lit up the yard in splotches. I could see the bushes move with the wind. A squirrel sat at attention waiting for something.

Momma didn't say anything about my new job, just let out a sigh. A little grin came to her face. "I'll wait in the dining room," she said after a minute.

"And I'll serve you like you are a queen."

She cocked her head like a bird. "Your granddaddy used to say that to me and Linda all the time. All the time when we were girls just your age. Just nine and twelve. Called us his queens."

"Really?" Her words kinda gelled up my guts some. Had Granddaddy told me what to say in my sleep? Whispered it from the past? From out of the closet? *She's a queen? My queen.* Had he said that?

I shook myself free of the cold sensation. We had to get

moving. I had to. "Now *I'm* saying it." My voice sounded thin. "I'll have breakfast to you in a minute and then we can go and wait for the bus."

Momma nodded and stepped light-footed into the dining room.

I let my breath out in a slow puff. Real careful I opened the window a little just so I could hear the call of the frogs. I moved the curtain some so it hid what I had done. Then I went back to cooking.

In a few minutes I took Momma's breakfast to her and set it on the dark wooden table. The room had a closed feeling—tight and hot. But the food made the air smell yummy.

"Mmm," Momma said. She looked up from the paper that was spread in front of her.

"How'd you get that newspaper?" I asked. I set her plate down.

"Granddaddy gave it to me."

I peered around the room. "You didn't talk to him, did you?"

That's the last thing I needed. My grandfather poking his head in here at this time of day. Especially seeing the plans Momma and me had. He sure could mess things up. Sure could. He sure *had*.

Momma shook her head and with her fork picked at the pancakes. Her hands, I noticed, shook. I poured the maple syrup for her, watching the pat of butter that sat in the middle of the pancake flatten out and follow the syrup down onto the blue plate.

"Eat a lot," I said. "You wanna make sure you got enough energy to make it through the day. And eat those eggs. You need the protein."

The Gainesville Times covered half the table. I knew without looking that my mother had been reading the section that talks about catastrophes near and far. She seemed all right, though. Not too jumpy. Not ready to head back to bed. Just a little worry rimming her eyes. Shaking in her hands.

Please.

I settled into the chair right next to her and started in on my food.

"Are you going to be fine without me?" she asked after a moment.

I looked up into her wide eyes. All of us, Momma and me and Aunt Linda and even Granddaddy have the same color eyes—dark like a troubled sky. Momma leaned toward me and smoothed my face with her hand. "You going to be able to do it?" Her hand was silky and cool. Gentle on my face. Tender.

I held still and let her pet me a moment. I closed my eyes to her touch and imagined her like somebody's momma from school. *She's like any other person,* I thought though I knew it wasn't true at all.

"Will you be fine?" she asked again. She moved away, settling her hands on the table, like a bird resting.

"Yeah," I said. I nodded. Tried to swallow. If spit wouldn't go down would food? "I'll be great." I cut at a pancake that was spread thick with soft butter. For a moment I remembered my aunt in here with us. All of us. An old memory. The way we threw back our heads to laugh. I couldn't have been more than five. All that laughter.

"What about you? Are you going to be okay? Should I go to work with you?" I asked. *Hope not. Hope not.*

"Me?" she said.

That one word came out so lean I could almost hear Momma's fear in it.

"Yes, you," I said, and fixed my eyes onto her face. All of a sudden I wasn't so sure I should leave her. Would Momma be okay alone? She hadn't done any wandering since those first few weeks after Aunt Linda left. And I always found her. That was more than a year ago. But . . .

Momma swallowed a few times. Did swallowing trouble run in the family? She looked off over my head, like maybe somebody waited behind me. But there wasn't anyone there, I knew. I mean, I didn't feel anyone back there. Then she nodded, though her lips seemed thin and too pale. "Oh, I'll be fine. You know that. We always do good. Even with Linda gone."

No we don't.

"I know," I said.

Right at that moment it felt like fire ants ran a path through me. I love my momma like nothing else but I wanted out. I *needed* to be out. Before Granddaddy started pestering her again. Before he started pestering *me*.

Get us out, out, out.

Carol Lynch Williams, who grew up in Florida and now lives in Utah, is an award-winning novelist with seven children of her own, including six daughters. She has an MFA in writing for children and young adults from Vermont College, and won the prestigious PEN/Phyllis Naylor Working Writer Fellowship. *The Chosen One* was named one of the ALA's Quick Picks for Reluctant Young Adult Readers and Best Books for Young Adult Readers; it won the Whitney and the Association of Mormon Letters awards for the best young adult novel of the year; and was featured on numerous lists of recommended YA fiction. Carol's other novels include *Glimpse* and the forthcoming *Miles from Ordinary*.